The Friendly Air

By the same author

The Past Tense of Love
The Golden Collar
Mrs. Westerby Changes Course
The Corner Shop
The Fox From His Lair
Canary Yellow
Come Be My Guest
The Toy Sword
Honey for Tea
Six Impossible Things
The Yellow Brick Road
Shadows on the Water
I Love a Lass
The Lark Shall Sing
Money to Burn
The Cuckoo in Spring
Around the Rugged Rock
Enter Mrs. Belchamber
Sun in the Morning
Iris in Winter
Last Straw for Harriet

The
Friendly
Air

by

ELIZABETH CADELL

William Morrow and Company, Inc.

NEW YORK / 1971

The Friendly Air

Chapter
1

Gerald had arrived fifteen minutes ago, wet, cold and queru-
lous, his coat snow-flecked, his teeth chattering. He had
pushed a chair as close to the single-bar electric fire as it
would go and was still crouched in it, rubbing his hands in an
attempt to warm them. He had complained bitterly and at
length about the vagaries of April weather, the inadequate
heating in trains, the scarcity of taxis and the total failure
of his weekend mission; now he was telling Emma, not for
the first time, what he thought of the comfortless bed-sitting
room, the shabby house and the seedy district in which she
had chosen to live.

  She decided not to interrupt the flow. She placed hot coffee
laced with brandy beside him; sipping it, he regained something of his normal composure, but not until he had drained
the third cupful did he seem sufficiently restored to be able
to answer questions.

  "What went wrong?" she enquired.

  "Everything. Blasted waste of time, as I knew it would be.

I told my father it was throwing away time and money—my
time and my money—but he thought I might be able to make
her see reason. And—"

"And she didn't?"

"If you're going to start breaking in—"

"Sorry."

"Well, as I was about to tell you, I got to the village after
a damned cold bus ride from York—through a blizzard. Was
the weather as stinking as that here in London?"

"No blizzard. Just sleet and snow taking turns."

"When I got to the village, I couldn't find the house. When
I found it, I couldn't open the gate. When I finally got it to
move, I tripped on a loose flagstone going up the path to the
front door and fell flat on my face. I had to knock for some
time, and when she finally opened the door, she simply stared
at me and asked my name. When I told her I was Gerald
Delmont, she pretended she hadn't recognized me."

"Perhaps she hadn't. She hasn't seen you—"

"She saw me six years ago, when I was a guest in her house
up in Edinburgh. I don't consider I've changed out of all
recognition since then."

She thought that perhaps he had. When he came to
London from York, six years ago, he had been a soberly
dressed citizen favouring dark, conventional suits. Today, he
was the model on whom every man-about-town in his thirties,
who wished to know what was sartorially what, kept a careful eye. Long and lean, he had a kind of natural elegance; he
achieved, effortlessly and with style, a Regency-rake effect
that his friends aimed for but for the most part missed. His
hair, which was very fair, grew to his collar and arranged
itself in a slightly upturned wave. He could wear elaborately
frilled shirts, satin or velvet jackets and lace-edged cuffs and

create not an effeminate but a distinctly masculine, boots-and-spurs impression.

"Why would she pretend not to know you?"

"To make herself objectionable. If it was genuine, if it wasn't put on merely to annoy me, then all I can say is that she's more than halfway cracked—which, as I reminded my father, has been my opinion all along. She's been a nuisance for years. Now that she's got all this money, she's going to be more than a nuisance; she's going to be a menace."

Emma listened absently and without interest. Nuisance or menace, it had nothing to do with her; the matter was between Gerald and his father and an old woman she had never seen and, until recently, heard very little about. At this moment Gerald needed an ear, and she would lend him one, but there was no need for her to get involved.

"What she needs," he was saying broodingly, "is to be put into some quiet retreat with people who'll keep an eye on her and see that she keeps out of trouble. A home for crackpots. Rich crackpots."

"But I thought you said—"

"It doesn't matter what I said. If you'll be kind enough to listen to what I'm saying now, you'll learn what happened today. If you'd come up to Yorkshire with me, as I asked you to, you might have been able to get some sense into her, or out of her. But you refused."

"Yes, because—"

"Because it meant altering your plans by five days. You could easily have told those people—"

"No, I couldn't."

"I can't see why you're going up at all. You haven't been to Yorkshire since your grandfather died. In fact, you've said

more than once that there was nothing to go up for. So what
is this—a pilgrimage?"

"No. Simply a visit to the Braisteds."

"Why did you have to stay with them? Why not with my
father in York?"

"Because I wanted to stay in Dunsway, that's why, and the
Braisteds, in case you've forgotten, own the farm less than a
quarter of a mile from the house I was brought up in. If
you'd been going up for longer than a weekend, I would have
gone with you, but you said that was all the time you could
spare."

"It was more than I could spare. Incidentally, I asked you
to get my car out of the garage. Where is it?"

"Not ready. Something about a defective something or
other."

"I also asked you to go to my flat tonight and cook a decent
meal for me because I'd need it after spending two hours on
a bus and three hours in a train. But you refused to do that,
too."

"Yes, because—"

"Because Claud happened to be entertaining his current
girl friend and you said you'd feel in the way. Since you
would have been in the kitchen, which is the last place they'd
think of spending their time, I fail to see the point of your
objection."

She understood well enough that it was hunger, and not
cold or fatigue, that was the real cause of his irritation. He
was a moderate eater, but he liked his meals well-cooked,
well-served and dead on time.

"You don't want to have dinner here, do you?" she asked.

"No, I don't. But nothing," he stated flatly, "will induce me
to go out again in this weather, though God knows I don't

fancy sitting here watching you fiddling with a gas ring and a sink. Why couldn't you have had some food ready?"

"Because you said you'd never eat a meal in this room."

"Well, I've changed my mind. Is this all the brandy there is?"

"Until you bring another bottle, yes."

He swore under his breath, and she slid open the cupboard that concealed the stove and the sink and began the preparations for a meal. They were not extensive. She kept little food in the room, for she had nothing but coffee for breakfast, a substantial lunch wherever she happened to be working, and for supper on her return, cheese and biscuits and yogurt. For the weekend, she bought trays of ready-made dishes, and two of these she now slid into the oven, under Gerald's unenthusiastic gaze—diminutive meat pies flanked by limp-looking potatoes and an unidentifiable vegetable.

"Am I expected to eat that?"

"That or nothing," she snapped. "If you'd phoned me before leaving York, I could have made you something nice. Now stop complaining."

Watching her moodily as she worked, he found himself experiencing the confused emotions that the sight of her always roused in him. The strongest was surprise that he had asked her to marry him, instead of choosing a wife from the sophisticated set in which he moved. But his next reaction was invariably one of relaxation—she was so unruffled, so calm unless he drove her too far, so great a relief after the tense, hypersensitive, over-emotional people he encountered during his working and his leisure hours. He could also feel a touch of pride—was she not largely his own creation? He couldn't claim credit for her beautiful bone structure or her long, lovely legs or her unusual colouring or her perfect skin—

but who had noticed them before he had made her dress properly, and sent her to a decent hairdresser? He had ironed out her gaucheries, taught her poise. Compare what she looked like now with what she had looked like two years ago. It was exasperating to have to admit that in herself she had changed not at all, but he still hoped that one day he would succeed in rousing in her some faint stirring of social ambition.

"Shall I make a salad?" she asked.

He shuddered. "Nothing cold, for God's sake. The temperature in this room is arctic. How you can live here beats me."

She controlled her rising anger. "I've got used to it," she said.

"All those squalling women—"

"They've stopped squalling before I get home. I told you—the singing lessons only go on until five-thirty. Will you eat at the table, or shall I put your tray on a tray?"

He did not smile; her jokes seldom amused him. He ate all she gave him, her pie as well as his own, handed back the trays and lit a cigarette.

"Feeling better?" she asked.

"Physically, yes. Now I've got to worry about how I can get this problem sorted out."

"Why do you have to? It's your father's problem. If you do manage to persuade her to come to London instead of going to York, how do you know she won't get into your hair instead of his?"

"She has no claim whatsoever on me. The only claim she has on my father is the fact that he was married for a short time to a relation of hers—but she's always held him responsible for what she calls her disastrous mistake in leaving Edinburgh and burying herself in a bleak Yorkshire village.

She said she did it on his advice—and so she's felt entitled to badger him ever since on every matter, big or small, that she wants cleared up."

For the first time, Emma's interest quickened. She hung the dish towel on a hook, slid back the concealing panel and turned to look at him.

"Advice? You mean it was simply because he advised her—"

He frowned. "You don't listen. I've tried to make it clear that she's not a woman who'd take anybody's advice."

"But she did take his advice about leaving Edinburgh and coming down to York?"

"Yes, she did," he answered, gratified to find that she was at last evincing some interest in the subject. "It was about the only occasion on which she listened to him. But that's all ancient history. The only thing that concerns us now is to prevent her from—"

"You don't like talking about the beginning of it, do you?" she broke in. "Why on earth not?"

"Because I see no reason to rake up an episode that shows my father in a rather unfavourable light. It was all over six years ago, and—"

"I know that. What I'm asking you is what happened before it was over."

"I don't want to discuss it."

Her patience splintered. "Well, I do," she stated. "I'm sick of the way you've always skated round the topic. Six years ago, your father made a fool of himself. So what? Old men frequently do. I was eighteen at the time, an age at which you'd suppose a girl could be told some of the more sordid facts of life without swooning, but all I got out of my grandfather was the bare fact that your father had remarried. The

village talked, of course, and I had good ears. I listened to all
I could."

"Then you probably got a completely garbled version."

"I probably did. So ungarble it. Tell me the terrible truth.
Unveil your father's shame."

"*Shame?*"

"As you said, garbled. How can you get any help from me
in this affair if I'm not put into the picture?"

He hesitated. "Very well," he said at last. "I'll tell you
what happened, but I shall not, now or in the future, allow
you to—"

"—wallow. Mud, mud, glorious mud. Go on—tell me the
worst."

"There was no worst. It was simply a case of a man of
mature years losing his head over an attractive young girl."

"Where did he meet her?"

"In Edinburgh. He and I went up from York for the Edinburgh Festival. I was twenty-eight and working, as you
know, in my father's firm of lawyers. The hotels in Edinburgh
were charging what he considered inflated prices, so he was
pleased when a friend of his told him about a lady—an
elderly lady named Grantly, English, widow of a Scottish
baronet—who had a large house in Edinburgh and was prepared to receive one or two guests for the period of the Festival. Screened, of course."

"Of course."

"I resent your tone, and I don't like your insinuation that
my father's a snob. He—"

"—just likes carefully screened people round him. Do go
on," she urged impatiently, "and leave out the unessentials."

"After an exchange of letters, my father and I went up. It
wasn't at all what we'd hoped to find. The house was quiet

enough, but it was extremely uncomfortable. There was only one maid, and the food wasn't up to much."

"Cheap?"

"It was very expensive, but then—"

"I forgot. Scottish baronet's widow. So?"

"I went to concerts. My father preferred to go to plays. If our tastes had been similar, if I'd been with him more than I was, if he—"

"You sound like Kipling. Shouldn't the heroine enter at this point?"

"If you persist in—"

"Where was this attractive young girl?"

"Staying in the house—the only other guest. She was Lady Grantly's great-niece."

"How attractive?"

"She was rather small, very pretty, and had auburn hair. Her name was Morag."

He paused and brooded, and she went to join him at the fire. Reluctantly, he moved his chair an inch or two farther away from it, and she brought a footstool and sat at his feet. This was the time, she mused, when couples coupled—united after absence, warmed and fed, with coffee bubbling at the end of its electric tail. This was the moment for him to seek response from her relaxed body. Who wrote all those books and plays about characters jumping the matrimonial gun? she wondered. They'd never met Gerald. But even if he did decide to jump, he wouldn't dream of jumping in this room, which acted on him like an extinguisher. And while his cousin Claud continued to entertain a succession of women in the flat they shared in Chelsea, he couldn't jump there either, so she was probably fated to be that despised and derided commodity, a virgin bride—and she rather liked the

idea, she decided, though she wouldn't have cared to admit
it and risk being looked down on as under-sexed, instead of
being looked up to as over-sexed. There didn't seem to be a
norm.

"Was this Morag sexy?" she enquired.

"I suppose you could say so. She certainly tried to engage
my attention."

"You mean she chased you?"

"If you care to put it like that, yes. I don't have to tell you
that I was of a serious turn of mind."

"And still are. Then what?"

"The concerts took place at night. During the day, I went
round Edinburgh, which I had never seen before and which
I found extremely interesting. Its history—"

"I'll read up on it. You went to concerts, your father . . .
How old was she?"

There was a pause.

"She was seventeen," Gerald answered reluctantly at last.
"*Seventeen!*"

"And a half."

"And your father was fifty-nine. And a half. You were right
about mature years. It makes you think of those medieval
royal marriages. What on earth could she have—"

She stopped. "—seen in him?" Why ask? He was her godfather and she knew the answer, and knew very well what a
sexy seventeen-year-old would have seen. Tall, well-pre-
served, handsome, with crisp grey hair, blue, quizzical eyes,
a kindly manner. He seemed ageless; since his retirement, he
had taken to making frequent trips to London; on each of his
visits, Emma looked for signs of change in him, and found
none. He looked like an archdeacon, which was probably
why he had chosen to retire to an historic little house in the

very shadow of York Minster, a layman in an ecclesiastical setting, discreetly wealthy, respected, pitied for that brief episode during which a scheming girl had taken advantage of him.

"Go on," she prompted. "You were enjoying the concerts and didn't see what was going on. But where was the great-aunt? Where was the Scottish baronet's widow?"

"Lady Grantly was never at home. If you believed her, she was running the Festival single-handed. That left my father and Morag together, and nobody knew the first thing about the affair until they announced that they were engaged and were going to be married without delay. You can imagine my feelings!"

"Never mind your feelings. Proceed."

"They were married in Edinburgh, and then they came back to York, to my father's house—which by that time I had left."

"Weren't you at the wedding?"

"I was not. I wasn't even in York when they got back. I'd transferred myself to a firm of lawyers in London. The marriage lasted four months. Then she found a younger man and went off with him. My father felt nothing but relief."

Humiliation too, Emma thought. He wouldn't have enjoyed the role of deserted husband.

"So how did the great-aunt, Lady Grantly, get to Yorkshire?"

"She made more fuss over the affair than all the other relations put together. She said that my father had ruined her position in Edinburgh. The parents were very well-connected and influential, and she said that they blamed her for everything. So my father advised her to sell her house and live near York. He arranged the sale of her house and found her a cottage in Oatfields, which as you know is unfortunately only thirty miles from York. She's been there ever since, and she probably wouldn't have dreamed of leaving if this money hadn't gone to her head. As it is, she decided to buy a house in York and picked out one next door to the one my father's been settled in so comfortably for the past two years. She was nuisance enough when she was thirty miles away, but if she comes to live next door, he'll have to move. He couldn't stand it. That was why he appealed to me—to us—to try and persuade her to find a house in London instead. And that was why I spent a freezing weekend up there, achieving exactly nothing."

"She couldn't have been poor before she got this money. Didn't you say she owned a large house and—"

"Too large, and completely out of date. It sold very badly. Her husband hadn't left her much—that was why she supplemented her income by taking in occasional guests. My father advised her to invest the proceeds of the Edinburgh house, but before he could advise her what to buy, she'd made her own decision and bought a packet of Terrazone shares—a tin mine God only knows where. She gave some of them to my father and his wife soon after they were married, but as they weren't worth the paper they were printed on, my father advised his wife to sell them at once."

"And she did?"

"Yes." He made the admission reluctantly. "She did. Two hundred shares in a tin mine which turned out . . . Two hundred shares which would have sold a month ago at . . . What the hell's the use of thinking about it?"

"Is Lady Grantly crowing?"

"No. She's too busy making plans to move. If you'd gone up with me, we might have talked her out of it. You could have met her as my future wife, we could have said we hoped she would consider moving to London instead of to York, we could have explained that we ourselves would soon be house-hunting and would put her in touch with any houses that might suit her. But you wouldn't come, and so she's still fixed on York."

"What exactly did you say to her today?"

"Nothing. She doesn't wait for anybody to say anything. She began, as I told you, by pretending not to recognize me. She went on to make disparaging remarks about my father. When I mentioned my engagement, she said that you had obviously not consulted the cards."

"The what?"

"Cards."

"What did she mean by that?"

"God knows. I didn't ask her—I didn't know how tangled it might get. She told my father that the cards had put her on to Terrazone. You see what I mean by being cracked? She was odd enough when we first met her, but I daresay her great-niece's marriage, her great-niece's subsequent divorce and her own recent lucky streak has all added up to send her over the edge."

"What's the house in Oatfields like?"

"Small, bleak, stuffed with furniture, most of it rather good. I would have liked to buy a couple of pieces. In fact, I suggested it, and wished I hadn't. She—are you listening?"

"Yes and no. I was thinking."

"Thinking about what?"

"Going to see her."

For some moments he was unable to speak. He turned in his chair and stared at her.

"Going to . . . going to . . . What the hell does that mean?"

"I thought I'd pay her a visit while I was up in Yorkshire, that's all."

"That's all? That's all? After having refused to go—"

"Don't let's go over all that again. Use your head. For years you and your father have shied away from any mention of Lady Grantly. As it was nothing to do with me, I didn't mind how much you shied. But now you've got me interested. Put it down to your gifts as a raconteur. You've turned her from a dim and rather dull figure into a real person, and I'd like to see her, even if it's only to ask her what she meant about the cards."

"And you couldn't have come with me?"

"No. Anyway, all you wanted me to go for was to bully an old woman and—"

"*Bully?*"

"Persuade. Advise. Bully."

"Look here, I've had enough of this. I'm going."

"You haven't drunk your coffee."

"I don't want my coffee. This is the kind of thing you're always doing—refusing to cooperate, keeping well out of a thing, and then coming in at the last moment by a side door. To go and see her together"—he rose and jerked his coat off the hook on which he had hung it—"would have been reasonable. To profess interest now, to insinuate that you can do more on your own than my father and I have done . . . And anyway, you're too late. You'll be wasting your time. Goodbye. If I stay, we shall have a row, and if we have a row, I shall say things I don't mean."

"No, you won't. You'll say things you do mean. You've got a bit of pie on your blouse."

"Would you kindly—"

"Sorry. Shirt. I wouldn't put that scarf on, if I were you. It's damp."

He crumpled it up furiously and thrust it into his pocket. He opened the door, backed away to allow an old lady to cross the landing on her way to the bathroom, and turned for a last word.

"When are you going up?"

"On Wednesday. I'll be back on Saturday, unless there's a snow block."

"And you're serious about going to see Lady Grantly?"

"Serious? I thought it might be amusing."

"Amusing is the last thing you'll find it. I can't think why the hell you want to do it. What have you and she in common?"

Emma did not tell him.

Chapter
2

Boarding the train at King's Cross on Wednesday morning, Emma thought that she could hardly have chosen a worse time for travelling. A long, dreary winter had been succeeded by a bleak spring. There had been April showers, but they had been of snow or sleet. Now April was in its second week, but there was no sign of warmer weather to come. The sprinkle of snow that was falling as the train drew out of the station grew heavier on the journey north; it settled on the windows and at last blocked the view.

She had no need to look out. She had made the journey to and from London many times in the past; she knew every station and every change of scene, from the last view of the Minster and the plains round Selby and Doncaster, to the bustle of Grantham and Peterborough and the series of tunnels that ended in the noise and confusion of London.

This time she was leaving London behind her and going up to the comparative calm of a cathedral city. She knew York as she knew the face that looked back at her each day from her mirror. She knew its Minster as well as any professional guide. She knew its streets, its gates, its history, its monuments. She had attended one of its schools as a weekly boarder, going back by bus every Friday to her grandparents' home in the moorland village of Dunsway, returning every Sunday evening to York. She had explored Fountains Abbey and Bolton Priory and she had picnicked in the ruins of Byland Abbey and Kirkham Abbey. She had played in Buttercrumbe Woods and braved the winds over Ilkley Moor and bathed in the cold summer sea at Robin Hood's Bay. All her youth was in Yorkshire, and the memory of her grandparents. Of her parents she had no recollection, for they had died before she was three.

All her youth? She had been young when she left—twenty. She had not wanted to leave. She had wanted to go to York, but her godfather, Mr. Delmont, had advised her to go to London, and she had taken his advice.

Advice to an unsophisticated girl of twenty. Paternal, kindly advice. With her grandfather lying in his newly made grave beside the almost as new grave of his wife; with the future terrifyingly uncertain, advice. You must get away, my dear Emma. You have been wonderful, quite wonderful in doing your duty by your grandparents, but they are dead and now you must begin to live your own life. Not here in Dunsway. This house is too large, this village is too far, this sphere is too narrow. And no, not in York. You have grown away from your friends, you have been shut up with old people, now you must get right away. To London. I will arrange the sale of the house, I will do this and that, I will write to my friends in London, you may rely utterly, and you must remember that Gerald, almost an older brother, is in London;

he will look after you. I am not only your godparent; I am now your only parent, lean on me and take my advice.

Well, she had taken it, hadn't she? she mused, and leaned over to make a small area of clearance on the misted window. But the snow still blocked the view, and she could see nothing, so she could go on thinking about those two first terrible years in London, when she had struggled, alone and friendless, to keep herself on the tiny income inherited from her grandparents and pay for some kind of training that would equip her for some kind of job. *I will write to my friends.* He may have, but none of them had troubled to look her up. *Remember that Gerald is there.* Yes, he was there. He had even taken her out to lunch shortly after her arrival, but once had apparently been enough; he had not repeated the invitation.

Advice. Nobody should ever be given advice. Nobody should ever take it, even if they believed, as she had believed, that it was good advice. She had learned, slowly and painfully, that it had been the wrong advice—but only when Gerald had been speaking the other evening of his father and Lady Grantly had it struck her that it had perhaps not even been disinterested advice. For her godfather, in advising Lady Grantly to go and live in London, was merely concerned with ridding himself of a possible source of trouble. An old woman who was threatening to upset his comfortable way of life . . . a young goddaughter who, if she stayed in York, would have to be watched over, placed in a job, entertained. . . .

She would never know the truth, she told herself, and perhaps she didn't want to. She had grown up. She had learned enough to know that the godfather she had loved and trusted was not a real figure, but one she had created for herself. Now that she could see him as he really was, it was amusing to watch him continuing to pose for her, still paternal, still kindly—and still handing out advice.

And now she was on her way to Yorkshire, and it would be interesting to see the village in which she had lived for so long—but it would be even more interesting to meet Lady Grantly, who, like herself, had had the doubtful benefit of Mr. Delmont's advice.

The train slowed; it was approaching York. It was no use trying to catch the first glimpse of the Minster, for a blizzard was raging. When she emerged from the train and stood on the platform, she felt the familiar whip of cold on her cheeks and smelled the damp, clinging mist that was one of her girlhood memories of winter.

The station looked unchanged, the platforms were as she remembered them. And there was the Flying Scotsman. She paused to watch it, as she had done so often when she was a child, letting her mind follow it north or south, glimpsing the passengers and the chromium gleaming on the tables of the restaurant car.

She had promised Gerald that she would go and see his father, but she had refused to stay the night at his house, pleading the need for hurry, since she was to spend only three days in Yorkshire before returning to London. There were no porters on the platform and no taxis on the rank outside. It was not far to walk, but she wondered uneasily whether the mist would thicken and prevent buses from running to country districts. With relief she saw that the snow had ceased to fall.

She crossed the wide street, suitcase in hand, walking slowly in spite of the cold that whipped her body. Under the bridge she saw the river Ouse, brown and sluggish—and there, ahead, half lost behind a curtain of mist, was the Minster, ghostly and beautiful. As she drew near, she could see the sweep of steps and the wide west door, and could picture the vast interior and the long line of choristers following the up-held Cross. Should she go in? Not now. She would have more time on the return journey.

The street in which her godfather lived was a cul-de-sac with houses on one side only—toy houses, sought after and select. She had not been here before; she had known him only in the house in which he had lived until his retirement—a large, ugly villa on the outskirts of the city, flanked by the residences of other successful lawyers. But she recognized easily enough the housekeeper who opened the door and, in broad Yorkshire accents, welcomed her and drew her inside.

"Come in, Miss Emma, come in." She closed the door and subjected Emma to a head-to-foot survey. "My word, you've grown! A good two inches. And the image of your grand-mother."

"You're looking very well, Mrs. Conder."

"Oh, I'm fine, miss, except for rheumatics. Gets me just here, in the shoulder blades. Mr. Delmont's had a touch of it too, but he's all right now. He's in his study—this way, miss."

She took Emma's coat, knocked on a door and ushered her in—to a room furnished with the same pieces, the same pictures and ornaments that had filled his study in the old house, so that she had for a few moments a dizzy sense of having slipped back to her school days.

He looked as fresh, as well-brushed, as beautifully groomed as always. His lips touched her offered cheek.

"Emma, how wonderful to see you up here at last! Four years—far, far too long. When Gerald telephoned to tell me you were coming, I thought he had made a mistake. Sit down here, close to the fire. What weather, what weather!"

"I like it this way. It reminds me of my school days, when the buses couldn't run and I had to stay the night at your house."

"You may have to do that again tonight; the mist will probably hold up traffic."

If it did, she thought, she would walk. No hard feelings— he was what he was, what he always had been; the only difference was that she couldn't be natural with him any more, and acting the affectionate goddaughter was tiring. It was a relief when Mrs. Conder wheeled in the tea things and waited, smiling, to be congratulated on having remembered all the old favourites: small round cheese biscuits, treacle tart, hot scones dripping with butter, fruit cake, honey cake, Yorkshire parkin. Emma ate with frank greed, not only to please Mrs. Conder but also to fortify herself against an almost certainly late arrival at Dunsway, with the bus crawling at a snail's pace through the mist, groping its way past dimly seen villages, stopping to pick up huddled figures that waited in the gloom.

When the tea things had been cleared away, Mr. Delmont settled back in his chair.

"There was something I wanted to ask you, Emma. Have you and Gerald fixed the date of your wedding?"

"Not finally. The middle of July, we thought."

"That's what I was afraid of. You see, any date in July will be quite impossible for me—I shall be in Italy, staying with the Paisleys. And for the whole of August, I shall be up in Scotland. I was wondering if it would be possible to arrange a date in September. I wouldn't dream of interfering with your plans, much less of asking you to put off your wedding day, if Gerald hadn't told me that you haven't yet found a house. If you remember, I advised you to wait until your house was ready before getting married—then you could go straight into it and settle down. But Gerald said—"

"Did he agree to a date in September?"

"My dear, how could he? He wouldn't agree without consulting you. You must discuss it with him when you get back to London."

September. In these surroundings, it was impossible to imagine herself married to Gerald. She could recall him as a tall, leggy youth helping her ungraciously into her school coat and making no secret of his relief at her departure. Then he was a spruce young man she met seldom, and always at his father's house. The last recollection in York was his impressive, white-tie-and-tailed presence at an official banquet. Then there was a long interval, after which he had appeared at the students' hostel in which she was living in London, in obedience to his father's request to look her up. He had looked her up—and down. Perhaps it was the look on his face, and the fact that he had left her as soon as politeness permitted, that made her take her first long, critical look at herself in a glass. When they met again two years later, he had barely recognized her, and this time he had not fled; he had taken her in hand and had completed the grooming process, and she had watched him as he became more and more interested in her, and then more and more in love, until at last his hesitations regarding her suitability were overcome and he asked her to marry him.

She had understood his qualms. He was enjoying great success, both professionally and socially. He shared with his cousin Claud a very large flat in Eaton Square, and to it Claud, a well-known producer, invited his famous friends.

They continued to come, for the two hosts made an original and interesting pair: Claud, short and stout and chatty and an authority on icons, and Gerald, tall, thin, terse, his clothes trend-setting, his outlook conventional.

Emma did not enjoy the parties. The guests were without exception from the stage or film or television world; she enjoyed looking at them and listening to them, but she could not share Gerald's opinion of their importance. To her, they were entertainers, paid by the public to perform; the better they performed, the more the public had to pay. All she felt in Gerald's drawing room was the satisfaction of seeing a free show. But she was learning to keep her opinions to herself.

When she left her godfather's house, she refused his offer of telephoning for a taxi; she would walk, she said.

"Have you changed your mind about going to see Lady Grantly?" he asked.

"No."

"Then I'm very grateful to you. It's more than kind of you to give up time on this short visit. Let me advise you, Emma, on how you should approach her. She's very odd, you know, very odd indeed."

"So Gerald said."

"Did he tell you what I've endured since she came to live in Yorkshire? Every time she has a problem, she writes to me—long and sometimes abusive letters. She uses my services as a lawyer and insults me when I send in a bill. She attempts to draw me into all her disputes—with the tradespeople, the village people, with anybody and everybody. And to propose to come and live next door to me without so much as a word! If a friend of mine hadn't been in the real estate agent's and overheard their conversation, I shouldn't have known anything about it. Do what you can to get her to London, I beg you, Emma. You're staying with the people at the farm, aren't you?"

"The Braisteds, yes."

"You'll find your grandparents' house quite changed; in fact, unrecognizable. I believe it's on the market for the third time since your grandfather died."

She left the house and made her way to the bus station. She had no need to worry about the mist; it was clearing rapidly, and the country buses were running. How many times, she wondered, had she come this way, how many times had she grasped the rail and swung herself onto the Dunsway bus?

By rubbing away the steam from the window, she could keep track of the route. Blocks of flats where once there had been fields. A factory and then another. A view of the new university. And then at last open country, a steep rise, narrow, snow-covered lanes and the crossroads with the signpost marking Dunsway.

They were waiting for her—the farmer, his wife and the two children who still remained at home. It was too dark to see her old house.

"You'll see it tomorrow morning from your bedroom window," Mr. Braisted told her, "but you won't recognize it. Been fair mucked about, it has. And this lot's leaving, same's the other two lots did. Too quiet 'ere, they said, and likewise too noisy—would we keep the cocks and the 'ens from waking 'em up, like, and would we stop the donkey from braying and the dogs from barking and the tractor from making that nasty noise. Proper town dwellers, the lot of 'em, what never should have come in the first place."

The view from her window on the following morning showed her nothing that she remembered. The house was a different house. The tangled garden had been tidied up and the gnarled old trees removed. The paddock was a swimming pool; the little glass shelter into which she had so often wheeled her grandfather's chair during his last months had been turned into a large conservatory. It was a strange house in a strange village that she had left long ago and had now, she realized, no desire to come back to. There was nothing to return to, no threads to pick up, no old ties to strengthen.

After breakfast she asked the farmer for the loan of one of the three work-worn cars lined up in a shed; the journey to Oatfields was easy by car but long and complicated by bus.

"I'll let you have the old station wagon," Mr. Braisted told her. "She's not smart, but she runs steady. The kids have been taking her round the big field, having a bit of driving practice, and it didn't do her paint much good. Grantly? Grantly? Can't call the name to mind. There was an old party at one of them bazaars last summer, making a fair dust-up because the flies wasn't being kept off the refreshments. She 'ad a name like Grantly, but maybe it wasn't the same."

Emma thought it probably was the same, and tested the brakes.

"You might find 'em a bit sharp, but that's better than t'other way round. Which way were you thinking of going? It's shorter by Nether Dunsway, but you'll likely come to grief on them slippery turns. You stick to the long way."

Sticking to the long way, she came to Oatfields, which she had in other days often passed, but never paused to inspect. This morning, with an occasional spatter of sleet cutting viciously across the pavements, with slush spinning from the wheels of passing cars, it presented a sight so drab and so grim that Emma wished she had stayed in the warm, comfortable farmhouse. Her interest in Lady Grantly diminished.

It would have been enough to remember her as somebody who, like herself, had suffered under Mr. Delmont's desire to arrange her future; where was the need for a visit? But she had sent a letter, a few lines to say that she was visiting her old home and would like to call. She had better put in an appearance. Perhaps there would be nobody there; she had telephoned twice from the farm, but hadn't been able to get through.

The main street was almost empty and looked desolate. Another, branching off it, was busier, with a row of shops. A few women, hooded and booted, with shopping baskets, tramped stolidly in or out of the butcher's or the baker's. Emma stopped to ask one of them the way, received a surly answer and followed the directions past a line of dreary-looking cottages to a turning that led to a narrow, muddy lane.

There was only one house in sight. Emma drove up to it, stopped in front of the high, badly hung gate and got out to take stock.

It was a grey, single-storied stone house, square and squat, with a central, unadorned front door and small windows to right and left of it. Broken flagstones made a path to the door. Behind the building stretched fields, but in front there was only a narrow expanse of what in summer might be grass but at present was mud.

The windows were closed, as was to be expected on a day like this. But the front door was open a little way, propped open by a stone. At this sign of occupancy, Emma was seized by a feeling akin to panic—what was she doing here? But it was too late to go away. A voice had floated over the hedge that bordered the garden.

"Who," it demanded angrily, "now *who* has left that wreck

in the middle of my lane?" The voice rose. "Are you there, whoever you are? Kindly remove it at once. You are blocking the only approach to this house."

It was a high voice, authoritative but musical; each syllable was clearly enunciated. Emma stepped to the hedge and looked over it. A few yards away a woman was standing on tiptoe in order to bring her eyes above hedge level, and was indignantly scanning the lane. And though Emma had not come with any mental picture, she had not the smallest doubt that she was looking at Lady Grantly.

She was a little shorter than Emma and enveloped in a voluminous cloak. Her head was bare, her hair grey and short and wavy; her skin was clear and firm, and she had a short, slightly uptilted nose. She turned and saw Emma and came towards her, calling as she approached.

"Is that your station wagon? I wonder if you would most kindly take it away?"

"I will if you like," Emma said, "but I've come to call on you."

"What did you say?" High though the voice was, it had no touch of shrillness. "I didn't quite catch you."

"My name is Emma Challis. I wrote to you."

"You did?" The tone was dubious. "Are you sure? I am Lady Grantly and this cottage is—"

"I know. I'm Gerald Delmont's fiancée."

A mistake, she saw at once. Doubt left Lady Grantly's face and was succeeded by apprehension.

"He's not *with* you?"

"No. I'm by myself."

It was a ridiculous conversation to conduct over a hedge on a freezing day, but she had received no invitation to enter. The cloak had fallen open, and she could see an ample, tweed-clad figure that had outgrown the slim legs and ankles. There was a familiar look about the faded blue eyes under the tendrils of natural little curls—Emma realized that she was looking at another of those women like her grandmother, born to be waited on, living to cope with a world made for the young and strong, dying without ever having lost the vague air of one looking round for a bell they could press to summon assistance.

"If you've come with a message from him," came Lady Grantly's voice, calm and frosty and recalling Emma to the present, "may I say at once that it is of no interest to me whatsoever?"

Emma smiled.

"No message. Just me. Can't I come in?"

Lady Grantly stared at her for some moments and then, apparently reassured, came to the gate and, with Emma's help, opened it.

"Don't think me inhospitable," she said, "but I feel certain there's some mistake. But it's far too cold to stand talking out here. Shall we go inside?"

She turned and led the way to the house, sending words over her shoulder, a subdued chattering that reminded Emma of water tumbling over stones.

"I am not at all deaf, but I do seem sometimes to get a wrong impression when people are talking to me. I was quite sure you said you were that man's fiancée, but the idea is so preposterous that I must apologize to you for entertaining it for even a moment. I . . . are you still there?"

"Right behind you," Emma assured her tranquilly.

"I often find that—" She stopped abruptly and turned to face Emma. "Would you most kindly go back and pick up the milk bottle just beside the gate? *That* was why I came outside—I remember now. The milkman won't come to the door any more, because he fell down on that loose flagstone—oh, *please* be careful!—and made a terrible fuss. Thank you so much. Now we can go inside." She resumed her walk to the door. "The milk bottle broke and he said he'd lost a pint of blood, and not one *word* about the pint of milk I'd lost. People are odd, don't you agree? Come in. Will you close the door?"

Emma closed it and saw that the wire letter rack attached to it contained a number of circulars and letters—her own among them.

"Please don't take them out," Lady Grantly requested. "I always like to leave my post until Sunday afternoons, and then I take everything out and read it at leisure. There's no hurry, you know; if there's anything urgent to tell you, people send a telegram, or use the telephone. It's very lucky that the postman still puts the letters into the box. I thought he'd stop, because one day—hang your coat there, will you?—one day he forgot to stoop as he was coming up the path, and a branch of the rosebush swept off his hat and scratched his face. I happened to be looking out of the window just then, and I was astonished to see a postman's hat suspended from a rosebush, just like the kind of thing you see in modern paintings. Shall we go into the drawing room?"

Emma, about to go in, hesitated. On a table by the door stood a telephone, its receiver laid beside it.

"Were you talking to somebody?" she asked.

"Yes, to you. I said shall we go into the drawing room?"

"I meant were you in the middle of telephoning to somebody?"

Lady Grantly smiled indulgently.

"Now, how could I possibly be?"

"The receiver's off."

Lady Grantly, taking a step forward and investigating, looked annoyed.

"Now, that's not where it goes," she said. "It's supposed to rest on its little cradle—like this." She paused in the act of replacing it and gazed with dawning horror at Emma. "You don't suppose, do you," she asked in a whisper, "that someone's still there?" Ear to the receiver, she listened and then replaced it cautiously in its proper place. "I couldn't *hear* anybody."

"Were you in the middle of phoning when you went outside?"

"I haven't touched that telephone," Lady Grantly declared, "since I answered it yesterday when Mrs. Ormskirk telephoned to ask me . . . oh, *that* was it! Thank goodness I've remembered. She wanted to know the time of the bus I catch when I go into York. I said I'd look it up, but something must have distracted me. It's all right; she won't want it now, because I remember her saying she couldn't go in today. Now let us go into the drawing room and make ourselves comfortable."

The room, like the hall, was full of beautiful furniture, polished and gleaming. There was no dust and no litter; all was neat, but could not be called tidy, since piece jostled piece, making it difficult to move across the room. By an electric fire no bigger than the one in Emma's room, Lady Grantly had made herself a small circle of comfort—her chair, a little bookcase, a low, circular table on which to put her work.

"I can see," she told Emma happily, "that you're a lover of nice things, and I have some lovely things that I can't bear to part with, so that's why everything's so crowded. Choose a chair you like, and bring it here to the fire. Are you comfortable? I was just sorting some of my old embroidery designs. I used to do the most exquisite work—all those chairbacks you see are the ones I did myself—but I don't have very much time for it now, because I have no servants except the two women who come in and do the floors and the windows and so on. If you can't find anybody who'll treat your things properly, it's far better to look after them yourself, and that's what I do, and I get very irritated when people tell me that if I sold half my things I would only have half the work. A man who was here the other day had the *effrontery* to make me an offer for that pair of little tables over there. Imagine walking into someone's house and behaving like an auctioneer! I always feel—I'm sorry; I interrupted you."

"I was only going to say that he was—"

"Did you come by bus, by the way?"

"No. I came—"

"Then that station wagon outside is yours?"

"No, it isn't mine. It—"

"Then *who* could have left it there? Not that man again? No. He couldn't possibly come back again after what I said to him. Would you like me to make you some coffee? It's so very cold outside."

"No, thank you. I was going to say that—"

"The reason I asked about the bus was that if you'd come by one, you would have found that they now stop just at the top of this lane. They never used to, you know. I used to have to walk all the way to the chemist's shop, where there was a sign. Can you imagine anything more ridiculous? '*This* is where I want the bus,' I said to them"—she stabbed a table with a forefinger—" 'here at the top of this lane, and not at the chemist's shop.' If I had my way, I would take down all those absurd signs and let each person have a little one of his own, to hold up when he wants the bus to stop. How can the bus authorities know exactly where people want to get on? It's the same with the pedestrian crossings. Now have you ever, *ever* found a pedestrian crossing where you want it? No. You have to walk several hundred yards one way or the other. But what were we talking about before I lost the thread? I do sometimes, you know; you must help me to find it again."

"I was going to tell you that the man who came to see you the other day, Gerald Delmont, was—"

"My dear girl, how amazing that you should guess! Do tell me, has he walked into your house, or your parents' house, and made offers for the furniture?"

"No. He—"

"He may well, he may well. I don't like to speak ill of anybody, but I've known both him and his father for many years, and the son is more objectionable, if possible, than the father. Let's talk about something more pleasant. Did you say your name was Emma? My mother's name. You're really an enchantingly pretty girl."

As you must have been once, Emma thought, with those eyes, and that lovely skin and naturally wavy hair and those delicate wrists and ankles.

"I really must make one point clear," she said. "I'm engaged to Gerald Delmont. He and I are going to be married in two or three months."

There had been so unbroken a stream of sound in the room since they entered that the silence resulting from this disclosure seemed to Emma unnaturally prolonged. Lady Grantly appeared to have been struck dumb.

"No!" she brought out at last, on a low, shocked note. "You can't be serious."

"Yes, I am."

"How in the world could a charming girl like yourself choose a man like that?"

"He's . . . well, he's been very kind to me, and I've known him all my life."

"You don't marry a man simply because you've known him all your life and he's been kind to you. For one thing, look at his extraordinary clothes."

"They're not extraordinary in London. Men copy them. In fact, Gerald thinks that men's clothes are going to get more colourful and women's clothes more plain—which he says is the way Nature intended it."

"My dear Emma, that's complete nonsense. He's thinking of peacocks. They may have to spread their tails to attract the females, but in this day and age a man doesn't have to dress up and strut. Any woman he wants is there ready for him, gift-wrapped. Did this man pester you to marry him?"

"No, of course not. We both live in London, and we saw a good deal of one another and—well, that's how it happened."

"Then the whole thing," Lady Grantly said, wringing her hands in distress, "is my fault. I am to blame."

"Tell me how," Emma invited gently.

"It was on my account, or rather because of a young relation of mine, that he went to London in the first place. If he hadn't gone, he wouldn't have met you. If he hadn't met you, you couldn't have become engaged. So you see? My fault."

"You mean because Morag married his father?"

"You've heard about it?"

"Yes. Your niece—"

"My great-niece. I suppose you heard the story from Mr. Delmont or his son. Their version, let me tell you, is inaccurate, prejudiced and—"

"You don't know their version," Emma pointed out.

"I know *them*. They probably blamed me for the whole thing. But how could I know that he would lose his head over a brainless little chit like Morag? To this day, I cannot understand how a man as vain as he was could have allowed himself to be caught in a situation in which he looked so ridiculous. I can only think that Morag must have threatened to make a fuss—but my goodness, in the end there was fuss enough."

"Why so much?" Emma asked.

"Blood. Blood, Emma. Blue, of course. I daresay you know that all true Scotsmen declare themselves to be directly descended from Robert the Bruce—though in my history books, all Robert the Bruce appeared to do was sit and watch spiders crawling up walls. Well, Morag's parents rather look down on Robert the Bruce. They claim descent from Malcolm, who, if you remember, was the son of Duncan, who was murdered by Macbeth in that Shakespearean play. They enact the whole thing every summer in that frightful draughty castle of theirs, all so gory. They sent Morag to me not, as you might think, to enjoy the Festival, but to choose the dress for her coming-out ball, after which her parents expected to interview a stream of suitors, royal or ex-royal. You can understand how they felt about a Mr. Delmont, old enough to be her grandfather, whom nobody had ever *heard* of. When it was all over, he advised me very strongly to come down to Yorkshire. He offered to see to everything—the sale of my house, which I never should have left, even if it was old-fashioned and much too large and very expensive to keep

up. Never did I imagine that I would find myself in this
grim little village and this horrid little house. I must have
been out of my mind, but when someone urges you to do
this and that . . . well, I gave in and here I am. And Gerald
Delmont went to London and now you're entangled with
him and we must get you disentangled as soon as possible.
How long are you going to stay in Yorkshire?"

"Only until the weekend. I've got to work next week."

"What sort of work do you do?"

"Fill-in secretarial jobs. I fill in for secretaries who are ill
or on holiday. I'm a stop-gap for firms who are replacing
staff. I did it, at first, because I wasn't trained to do anything
else, but I found it paid well, so I went on doing it. They send
you a slip every Friday telling you where you're to report
on the following Monday. If I want a week off—like this
week—I take it. I can earn a bit extra by taking jobs in which
I can use my Spanish."

"You speak Spanish?"

"Yes. Night school."

Night school. Two words that bridged, she realized now,
two phases of her life. Lonely and miserable in London, she
had begun to study. She had brushed up on her French and
she had achieved a high degree of proficiency in Spanish,
and in doing so, had found friends, fellow-students who for
the most part dispersed at the end of the sessions, but in
whose company she had recovered her self-reliance and lightness of spirit.

"I used to speak excellent French," Lady Grantly was
saying, "but I daresay I've forgotten most of it. Have you
been to Spain?"

"I've never been anywhere. I was brought up in Dunsway,

not far from here. Mr. Delmont, Gerald's father, is my god-father."

"In that case, it's going to be more difficult than I thought to get you out of his son's clutches. When he mentioned a fiancée the other day, I did send some kind of message of warning, but I don't suppose he troubled to give it to you."

"He said something about cards. What did that mean?"

"Exactly what it sounds like, my dear Emma. If I had consulted the cards before coming down to Yorkshire, I should still be in my house in Edinburgh. But I didn't, and as you see, here I am."

"What sort of cards?"

"Ordinary, everyday cards. Playing cards. If you follow certain rules in setting them out, if you believe the answer they give you, you can save yourself from making a good many serious mistakes in life. I can't *tell* you what they've done for me! Have you heard that I now have a great deal of money?"

"Yes. The Terrazone boom."

"Mr. Delmont can't even *talk* about it without raising his blood pressure. You see, he advised me to buy shares with the money that I got from the sale of my house. So I got out the cards when he had gone away, and the answer that came out was T and Z. I went at once to my bank manager, and he found lots of shares with T, but the first T *and* Z we got to was Terrazone. The bank manager didn't want me to buy them, I can't think why, because they were very cheap. I did buy them, quite a lot of them, and I gave some of them to Mr. Delmont and Morag, but he said they were worth nothing and advised her to sell them, which she did. He thought they were worthless simply because they were at a low ebb, but as I pointed out to him, how could I have got them so cheaply if they *hadn't* been? Everybody who knows the first thing about shares and so on should know that you *must* buy them *before* they go up. Which is what I did. And you must *not* sell them *until* they go up. That was the mistake Mr. Delmont made, but he didn't behave very well when I told him so. He asked me where I'd learned about them, and when I told him that it was from the cards, he hinted that I was demented. So I shall certainly not tell him that I consulted the cards again when I got all that nice money. They said I was to buy a house."

"Did they say where?"

"No. They don't tell you *everything;* they give you a lead and then you must decide the rest for yourself. But I didn't want to go back to Edinburgh, so I thought I could get myself a really warm, comfortable house in York. I went to a real estate agent and I found this nice— Were you going to say samething?"

"I was going to ask why you chose a house next door to Mr. Delmont's."

"Next door to . . . Emma, what a *fantastic* notion: Mr. Delmont lives in one of those dreadful villas out on the—"

"He moved."

"I didn't know that. Where did he move to?"

"Next door to the house you're buying."

"Next door to . . . You mean to tell me that he has actually moved to a house in which he would be my *neighbour?* No, Emma, you've made a mistake. If there's one thing that he would loathe more than I would loathe being next door to him, it would be being next door to me."

"Well, he is. I mean, he will be."

"Then I shall do all I can to prevent it."

"You can't. I saw him yesterday. He's—"

"Next door!"

"Yes."

"You're quite, quite certain?"

"Quite."

"Then I shall cancel the whole thing. I shall go and see the real estate agent and I shall—"

"Did it have to be York?"

"Did what have to be York?"

"This house. If you're going to move, couldn't you move to London?"

And that, she realized with amazement, was exactly what Gerald and his father had asked her to say—but she had not spoken on their behalf. The words had been the culmination of all that she had been feeling since she had arrived here. She could not have said whether she considered Lady Grantly entirely normal, but crazy or not, she liked her. She liked the look of her, she liked the flute-like voice, the mixture of sense and nonsense, the intriguing blend of silliness and shrewdness. She liked her, and she wanted to see more of her. Most of all, she wanted to . . . to what? Protect her. She was old, she had money, she was about to launch herself on the world, alone. People would think her odd and would either laugh at her or try to take advantage of her. Few of them would want to stay in her company, far less dream of enjoying it, as she was doing. Gerald had asked what she and Lady Grantly had in common, and now she could tell him that it was something more than having suffered under his father's advice. But if she tried to put her feelings into words, they would sound absurd; what would Gerald make of an assertion that she and Lady Grantly were kindred spirits? How could she explain that she felt completely at home in this old woman's company?

"London?" she heard her saying, and there was a note in
the voice that told her persuasion would be of no use. "No,
Emma; not London. All that *turmoil.* I never liked it, and I
should like it even less now that I'm old. Not London."

"And not back to Edinburgh?"

"No. I should never have left, but I shall never go back."

"Then where?"

"I shall put it to the cards. Whenever I find myself at a
loss, whenever I need directing, I invariably let the cards
guide me."

Emma said nothing. Lady Grantly walked to the window
and gazed out.

"Come and look, Emma."

Emma looked. The mist, descending once more, was shut-
ting out the view. The road had vanished, then the hedge and
the rosebush on which the postman's hat had hung. Soon
there was nothing but greyness and gloom.

"Would you like me to switch on a light?" she asked.

"Yes, please. And draw the curtains and tell me how I
could have endured this for so long. You know, I was born
in Barbados, in the sunshine. Such a lovely house, such a
heavenly garden, such a view! My parents sent me to school
in England; it was a very expensive school, but they didn't
succeed in teaching me anything at all, except embroidery.
So when I was sixteen, I was allowed to go back to Barbados,
back to the sunshine. When I married, my husband's work
took him to India, and there was more lovely sunshine. I shall
get out the cards, and you'll see—they'll give me a lead to
some charming place where there are flowers all the year
round. Will you stay on and have a little lunch with me
afterwards?"

"Thank you. I'd like to."

"Can you cook?"

"Quite well, when I have to."

"Then you shall make an omelette and I shall whip up some little thing with fruit and cream. And there's cheese, and I have good coffee. It will be delightful to have you. And now I'll get out the cards. You must watch how I set them out."

Emma, watching, realized that Gerald would consider this a clear proof of insanity, and perhaps by some standards it was. But then who could have been more odd, towards the end of her life, than her own grandmother, who gave the birds names and titles, who never went past the little bust of Queen Victoria in the hall without curtseying, who decided to change her name to Ethelfleda and called her husband Ethelred? Nobody ever called her crazy, only eccentric. If Lady Grantly wanted to plan her future with the help of playing cards, why stop her? If it came to that, how? She was her own mistress and she could pay for her mistakes out of the Terrazone profits.

"Eight lines of four—are you paying attention, Emma? Cards face downwards. That makes thirty-two, and I'm left with twenty. Do you follow?"

"So far, yes."

"I learned this, you know, years and years ago, in Sark. There was a most evil-looking old woman who used to follow us—my husband and myself—whenever we went for a walk. One day, when I was alone, she came up to me and said that if I went to her cottage, she would tell me how to make a fortune. Well, we were always rather poor, so I couldn't resist going, although I felt a little nervous. When we got there, she asked me for five silver coins, and when I gave them to her, she taught me this way of setting out the cards.

I feel so sorry that the fortune didn't materialize until my husband was dead, but if he'd been alive, he wouldn't have let me spend it, so perhaps it's just as well. Now I shall show you what you do with the twenty cards that are still left. You put them out, face upwards, in lines of four—like this. There they are. Now what I must do is see what I can learn from them."

Silence fell. Lady Grantly counted, murmured to herself and turned the cards over, one by one. Emma, watching dreamily, had a feeling that she was floating in space, freed from a world of political parties, politicians, commentators and tycoons. She was about to join Gerald on the social tread-mill—round and round, and then round again—and again. But at this moment, September seemed a very long way away.

"Now, Emma."

She roused herself.

"You buy the house where?" she asked.

"*That* is what we are now going to find out. I've done all the preparation, but I don't think your mind was on it. Now we simply have to count."

"Count how many?"

"I don't know yet. Let me see . . . fifteen. No, sixteen. We have to count sixteen, and then we shall know the answer. What is the sixteenth letter of the alphabet?"

"Q. No, P."

"Are you sure? We have to make quite certain we don't make a mistake. This part is very important."

"It's P. How does that help us?"

"It's the *answer*, Emma, it's the *answer*. We must choose a country, and in that country I must buy my house."

"Don't you get told more specifically?"

"Certainly not. I told you that the cards don't do *everything*. Now, what countries begin with P?"

"Patagonia."

"Where is that?"

"I'm not too sure, but I think it's where South America tapers off."

"Where does it taper off to?"

"Doesn't it end up somewhere near Tierra del Fuego?"

"Tierra del Fuego?"

"Yes. But as I said, I'm not certain. Haven't you got an atlas?"

"I don't need an atlas to find out where Tierra del Fuego is, Emma. It's practically *touching* Cape Horn!"

"In a way, yes."

"Where all those poor sailors were wrecked."

"Not all of them."

"And a terrible, terrible climate, I read once."

"Not exactly salubrious, no."

"Is that the only country that begins with P?"

"Heavens, no. There are dozens, but I can't call any of them to mind. Yes, I can. Pakistan."

"I was out there years and years ago, with my husband. It was very pleasant, but I'm told it isn't at all the same nowadays. No, not Pakistan. Where else is there?"

"Couldn't it be a place, a town? There are some lovely ones beginning with P, like Paphos and Papua. As a matter of fact, I misled you, because I remember now—Patagonia is simply a region of Argentina."

"It doesn't matter. I'm not going there."

"Did you know that there are two places in Ceylon called Palampodder and Pallavarayankaddu? What could be nicer than Palampodder or Pallavarayankaddu? If you went there, I'd have to go with you."

"*Countries*, Emma, *countries*."

"Paraguay."

"Now, I've heard about that. Or was it Uraguay?"

"Both. Do you fancy Paraguay?"

"I don't think so. It has a kind of wild sound."

"There's another place in Ceylon called Pedrotallagalla."

"How on earth did you learn these extraordinary—"

"Night school. There was a girl from Ceylon who used to reel off names like those, and we were so sure she was making them up that we checked, and sure enough, there they were. Oh—Peru."

"No."

"Philippines?"

"Well . . . they're islands, aren't they, and I do love the sea. Can't you think of anything nearer home?"

"Portugal. How about Portugal?"

"Now *that* is what the cards had in mind." Lady Grantly sighed with relief and leaned back in her chair. "Tell me what you know about Portugal."

"I don't know anything whatsoever, except that it starts near Vigo and goes down and round the corner and finishes up—"

"I didn't mean geographically. I was thinking of the climate."

"I think windy summers and wet winters. I don't think that sounds comfortable, do you?"

"Wind, perhaps not. But rain . . . Do you know, Emma, I *love* rain."

"A shower now and then, maybe. But I think it starts

coming down about October in Portugal, and doesn't let up until the spring."

"So that when it stops, all the trees and the bushes must look fresh and new and beautiful. And there's a lot of sea, isn't there?"

"There's a long coastline, yes. But it's an Atlantic coastline. That's the catch, someone told me once. People go out there thinking it's Mediterranean, and it isn't; it's Atlantic, which means waves bashing on the beaches, and storms, and—"

"Are the summers warm?"

"Yes. And dry. Scarcely a drop of rain, as far as I can gather, between April and October. But wind, as I said. Very strong wind. And along the coast in summer, so my informant said, morning mist that doesn't clear until about eleven, making it pretty cool if not chilly."

"Are you trying to make me dislike Portugal?"

"No. You asked for information, and this is it. When I get back to London, I'll go to the Portuguese tourist office and . . . On second thought, I won't. Why would a tourist office give you a list of the drawbacks? I'll try and locate this friend, whoever she was, and jog her memory."

"Portugal. Imagine, Emma. Just a few days in a ship, and—"

"Two. What's wrong with flying? Two and a half hours."

"There you are, then. Perfect. Not too far, with sunny summers and rain in the winter, instead of fog and sleet and snow. You must do something for me as soon as you get back to London—find me a house out there, and then we shall go out as soon as we can."

"Not me. You."

"I would be very upset if you couldn't find a little time to go out there with me and help me to settle down. I would, naturally, pay all your expenses, and I would also make up to you the money you'd lose by giving up your work for a time."

"Thank you. But Gerald might have something to say if I announced that I was dashing off to what might have been Patagonia."

"Gerald?"

"You've forgotten. Gerald Delmont. I'm going to marry him."

Lady Grantly merely swept up the cards and replaced them in their case.

"Nonsense, Emma," she said. "Nonsense."

Chapter
3

Returning to London and reporting on her visit to Lady Grantly, Emma found herself regarded by Gerald with a new respect. To have achieved so much where he and his father had achieved nothing; to have succeeded in persuading this potential threat to their peace to remove herself not merely to London but all the way to Portugal; above all, to have returned with full authority to choose and buy a house, so that retraction would be all but impossible—how had she done it?

Emma thought it unwise to tell him that the cards had done it. She said little about her visit and nothing at all about its prolongment. She had stayed not only to lunch, but also to tea and supper. She had spent the night on the sofa in the drawing room, wearing a pair of Lady Grantly's Chinese pajamas. And on the following morning she had helped to open trunk after trunk full of clothes which had not been worn since Lady Grantly had accompanied her husband to official functions.

"You see, Emma, how wise I was not to have thrown or given away all these lovely things? This beautiful silk suit, for instance, and that lovely little shantung dress that people always remarked on when I wore it. This dress—let me spread it out so that you can see it properly—is one I wore at the Viceroy's Ball; I bought it in Paris and it was a great success. I've never been able to use it since, because it's rather *grande-toilette*, but I shall certainly take it out to Portugal in case I attend any official receptions there. What a pleasure, what a joy to see all these things hanging up again after having been hidden away in trunks for so long. Look at this linen suit—isn't it beautifully cut? However much fashions change, you can't go wrong if you have good cut and good-quality material. I put on weight shortly after I married, but I've never altered since, so that all these clothes I bought when I went out to India with my husband, all those years ago, will be perfect in Portugal."

Emma did not think that any of this would have been of interest to Gerald, nor would Lady Grantly's instructions about the type of house she had in mind.

"Not large, Emma; remember that. I'm sorry to give you this trouble, but it's far, far better for you to make the arrangements in London. A house with just enough room for you and me and the maids. Two maids, I think; they're company for one another. And a car and a chauffeur. These I *must* have, otherwise I shan't be able to get about. Oh dear me, how nice it is to be talking about a car and chauffeur again. How true it is that money can't make you happy, but it can make you very comfortable. It's so long since I've been really comfortable. I feel so grateful to those splendid cards for telling me about Terrazone. Just *think* where I should

have been if I had listened to Mr. Delmont instead of following the cards!"

"Go on about the house."

"I'm so sorry, I lost the thread again. A nice little house,
white, with a view of the sea. It needn't be right on top of
the sea—just a glimpse will do. And not too isolated, but *not*
in a residential district. Heaven preserve me from residential
districts! Some pleasant neighbours not too far away, so that
I could stroll over sometimes. Look, here's this beautiful
sunshade I used when I strolled round our lovely garden in
New Delhi. Isn't the lace exquisite?"

But the chief news item that Emma kept from Gerald was
her promise to go out to Portugal with Lady Grantly and
settle her into the small white house. This, she knew, would
have interested him very much indeed, but as it would have
upset him too, she persuaded herself that it would be charitable to postpone the revelation.

Her reasons for agreeing to go were not clear to herself, so
it would have been impossible to make them clear to Gerald.
Something in her had reawakened during the day and night
she had spent with Lady Grantly—her instinct to protect the
elderly and the aged, bred by the necessity of looking after
her grandparents, fostered by her affection for them. She
could not bear to think of Lady Grantly embarking alone
upon this adventure, and so she was going with her. She had
given her promise, but there was no need to tell Gerald . . .
yet.

He urged her to go without delay to a real estate agent.

"You can kill two birds with one stone," he pointed out.
"Our house and hers. Has she given you any definite figure?"

"No. But she doesn't want a large house."

"What would she want a large house for? Did she have any idea where in Portugal she'd like to be?"

"No."

"I'll have a word with Denys Clifford. He's just sold a house out there. He sold it, as a matter of fact, to Nancy Cooper. He— What's amusing you?"

"The combination of Sir Denys Clifford and Nancy Cooper."

"He wanted a lot of money for the place, and she was prepared to give it to him—what better combination could you have than that? As a matter of fact, it was rather a clever move on his part. He heard she was after a house close to his—far too close. He didn't want pop singers on his doorstep, so he got in touch with her and said that he was prepared to sell his, furniture and all, and she bought it. He's coming to the party that Claud and I are giving next week, so I'll have a chat with him about house prospects out there. And speaking of house prospects, we've got a much better chance of finding one for ourselves now that we've put the wedding off until September."

"Have we?"

"Have we what?"

"Put it off until September?"

"You should know. My father rang up just after you'd been talking to him, and told me you'd agreed to September."

"All we agreed was that I'd talk to you about it and get your views before deciding."

"Well, have you any strong objections to putting the date back?"

"No."

"Then why the fuss?"

"It doesn't seem much of a reason for postponing a wedding, that's all—just because your father's got a previous engagement."

"We'd only made a tentative date, and we made it before we decided that it would be wiser to buy a house than to rent one. Now we've at least got time to look round and find something that'll suit us, instead of rushing at it. I suppose you're annoyed because my father took my agreement for granted?"

"No. Because you took mine for granted."

"I can't see why—"

"I accept your apology. Who else is going to this party?"

"Party?"

"Yours and Claud's."

"Oh, the usual crowd. What are you going to wear?"

"The usual outfit."

"Why on earth can't you—"

"No. I'm saving up for my trousseau."

"My father told me he'd offered to pay for your trousseau and you'd refused. He was rather hurt."

"He didn't look hurt; he looked relieved. Weren't you going to take me out to lunch?"

The invitation had been a reward for the good work she had done on her visit to Lady Grantly. He decided to take her to a small restaurant he had discovered on the fringe of Soho and publicized with such success that the grateful management had responded by omitting to present a bill when he was alone or with a companion. He regretted the decision when he remembered that she always made lunch her principal meal. He watched her disposing of soup, scampi and a steak whose thickness and redness made him shudder, and wondered what the waiters thought of her too-healthy appetite. But there was no need to wonder; he knew that her natural, unaffected charm, which regrettably made so little impact on his friends, wrought havoc among waiters, bell boys, parking attendants and shop assistants. Perhaps it was as well that he had brought her here; if he had been paying, the bill would have been astronomical.

"Don't you ever think about your figure?" he enquired.

"Figure? Oh, you mean I'm eating such an awful lot? Well, I need building up—think of all those real estate agents I've got to tackle."

"I've got a list of them for you and I've marked some of the more suitable offers. I looked at a couple of them while you were away. If you find anything really promising, ring me up and I'll try to meet you so that we can look at it together."

"What about that house Claud mentioned?"

"It wasn't a house, it was a flat, and those people my father dislikes so much live above it, so that ruled it out."

"I don't see why. Anyway, they're clients of yours, aren't they?"

"No longer. They made difficulties over an account I sent them. I had to explain that I wasn't in business for fun."

"Who is? That's what's wrong with business. People . . . Goodness, this looks delicious. Aren't you going to have any?"

"Thank you, no."

"You don't know what you're missing. Who's that?" she asked, seeing him half rise and give a slight bow.

"Nancy Cooper plus the usual entourage. Don't stare, please."

"All right. But it's a shame not to be able to. I've never seen a pop star close to. She looks like a schoolgirl."

"In a different walk of life, she would be a schoolgirl."

"How old?"

"Sixteen."

"I didn't know you'd met her."

"Claud brought her into the office. She wanted me to do a bit of work for her. I turned it down."

"Why?"

"A bit off my beat, I thought. Besides which we didn't take to one another."

Emma ventured another discreet glance. Long fair hair, a plump little figure, a plump little face, round brown eyes, a small nose and a large mouth—through which had issued the song, written by her brother Leonard, that had won the nationwide television contest held six months ago, launching her to a success which seemed likely to be lasting. Born and brought up in the East End of London, her father a plumber, her mother an office cleaner, she had a fund of common sense and astounding poise. Emma thought her voice a mixture of sand and treacle, but enjoyed the unrehearsed interviews at airports or stage doors during which, her way barred by out-thrust microphones, she gave sensible answers to silly questions.

"Did you say she'd actually bought Sir Denys Clifford's house in Portugal, or that she was only thinking about it?" she asked Gerald.

"Bought it. She went out to see it. It's not for herself—it's for her parents."

"Didn't I read somewhere that she'd bought them a house in Surrey or Sussex?"

"I've no idea. Drink your coffee, will you? I've got to get back to the office."

"I was wondering if I could have—"

The waiter appeared at her elbow. "Yes, madam?"

"There's some of that lovely cheese over there that I can never afford to buy."

"Certainly, madam."

"Sheer greed," she said, watching him speeding to bring her what she wanted. "But do you know how much that cheese costs per quarter of a pound?"

"Yes, I do," Gerald said shortly.

"If you do, and if you know I like it so much, why don't you bring me some, instead of bringing chocolate pepper-mints?"

"I have yet to hear of a man who goes to visit his fiancée taking—"

"Why not? You're well known for making innovations in gents' wear; why not in other departments?

"Knock, knock, who goes there?

A lover carrying Camembert."

"Emma, don't sing!" he implored, writhing in embarrass-ment.

"Nobody heard. If they did, they thought it was Nancy. Oh, thank you. Is there by any chance an apple? Cheese and apple go so . . . Thank you."

"I don't want to cut this feast short," Gerald said coldly, "but may I remind you that although you've taken the week off to go house-hunting, I've got work to do?"

"Three minutes."

"And I'd like to know exactly what instructions Lady Grantly gave you."

"I'm to go to the London agents who have houses abroad, choose one that would suit her, buy it and then let her know."

"After which?"

"After which she'll come to London, stay somewhere near me and make all the final arrangements."

"I advise you to put all the final arrangements into my hands. If she's thinking of going abroad permanently, there'll be a number of things to see to. Bank of England permission, for one."

"She didn't say she was going abroad forever. She just wants to buy a house in Portugal, that's all."

"Does she propose to shuttle to and fro for the rest of her life?"

"Not exactly shuttle. All she wanted—"

"You mentioned two maids and a chauffeur. That sounds permanent enough to me. Whether she goes permanently or not, there are laws she'll have to observe. To my mind, it would be far easier if she declared herself non-resident at once and got permission for all her assets, or as many of them as they allow, to be transferred to Portugal."

"You mean be an expatriate?"

"Why not? She'll settle down in a house she likes, with servants to look after her, and that'll be the end of her as far as you and I and my father are concerned. I can tell you now that I wouldn't have been prepared to put up with much of her if she'd come to live in London. She— *What* did you say?"

"I said she was rather nice."

"Lady Grantly?"

"Yes."

"Are you forgetting that I've met her?"

"No. But she didn't like you either, so—"

"Oh, really? In what way, may I ask, did I offend her?"

"By offering to buy some of her furniture, and because you remind her of your father, who—"

"Oh, really?"

"Don't keep saying 'Oh, really.' All she meant was that you might get like him in the end."

"Oh, r . . . ? Am I all you found to discuss while you were with her?"

"Of course not. She didn't want to talk about you because she said she likes to be charitable. Did you know how much she got for those Terrazone shares?"

"Yes, I do."

"You should have told me. It made me feel dizzy. Couldn't I have some brandy with my coffee?"

"Certainly, if you want it," he said stiffly. "And before I mention houses to Denys Clifford, you'd better let me know exactly what details Lady Grantly gave you."

"White."

"Very helpful, indeed. Anything else?"

"I told you—smallish. And a sea view."

"That's going to be of great assistance to the real estate agents. Will you please hurry?"

She gathered her things together and led the way out between the tables. Then she stopped in dismay and turned. "Oh, Gerald, you forgot to pay the bill!"

"Go on, will you?" he muttered.

"But we can't go until—"

"Go *on*, I said."

"But—"

"There is no bill."

"You mean it was free?"

He took her arm and led her out into the street. "When will you learn," he demanded, "to—"

"Why didn't you tell me? I was longing to have lobster, but I didn't, because it's so expensive. How could you deprive me of lobster? Do restaurants often let you eat for nothing?"

"No, they do not."

"Well, next time, remember to tell me."

If, he thought bitterly, striding away after a curt farewell, if there was a next time. She was really impossible at times. It wasn't that he was too conventional, but there were limits. The trouble was that below the thin veneer of sophistication he had succeeded in giving her she had remained obstinately provincial. She remained, essentially, herself—a very attractive self, he'd freely admit, but not one that fitted well into his circle. It was not surprising that his choice of her as a wife had puzzled his friends; beside actresses famed for their beauty, her looks were not outstanding. She was not up to the intellectuals, not frothy enough for the featherheads. And she had never lost her unfortunate tendency to speak plainly; she had strong views, but they were the wrong views.

But then, he remembered, reaching his office and pressing the button for the lift, it was no use denying that she had some basic quality that seemed to restore or reassure him. Perhaps marriage to him would give her the touch of polish she so lacked.

He did not see her again until the night before his party, when she came to his flat to arrange the flowers. She had told him over the telephone that she had been going round the real estate offices, and he was looking forward to hearing how much progress she had made.

The living room of the flat was immense, with two of its four windows overlooking the square. The other rooms—two bedrooms and two bathrooms and a kitchen—were cramped by comparison. The layout was in direct contradiction to Emma's ideas on comfortable living; she would have settled for a living room a quarter of the size of this one, and given the space to a kitchen in which a husband could sit, relaxed and at ease, in an easy chair and slippers, talking to his wife as she prepared his meals. But Gerald into slippers didn't go.

He and Claud used the kitchen merely to prepare their morning coffee or when making themselves a snack in the evening. Neither of them had domestic tastes, neither of them cared for domestic women.

She came in from the kitchen with a vase full of water and put it on the marble-topped table on which she was arranging the flowers.

"I heard of a house today," Gerald told her.

He was lying in a Swedish chair watching her and telling himself that for this sort of thing she had a professional touch. He had dined early with his father, who had come to London for the day on business; after driving him to the station, he had returned to the flat.

"What sort of house?" Emma asked.

"Not too large, this fellow who was telling me about it said, and not too expensive. It sounded rather promising."

"Has it got a sea view?"

"*Sea* view?" He twisted in his chair and stared up at her. "*Sea* view? Who the hell has a sea view in London?"

"Oh—London!"

"Yes, London." He sat upright, swung his legs to the ground and spoke with force. "London. London, England. Where we both live. Where we propose to go on living when we're married. London, in which I've supposed you to be trying to find a house for us. Do I understand that all you've been doing for the past week has been not on our behalf, but for this woman up in Yorkshire?"

"Two birds with one stone was what you said."

"So you devoted ninety-nine and a half per cent of your time to Lady Grantly and the residue to ourselves?"

She put a rose carefully into place and tried to subdue a feeling of guilt—his guess at the proportions was only too accurate. She had neglected his interests, and why? Because it had been far more fun to project herself into a future filled with sun and flowers and sea-fringed gardens than to plod round empty, echoing, town houses flanked by other town houses and looking out onto still more town houses.

"Well, isn't it?" she heard Gerald insisting. "All for her and nothing for us?"

"If I don't find her a house, who will?"

"Didn't she find one without difficulty in York? Why can't you understand that she's a rich woman, well able to—"

"You knew I was going to look for a house for her. You even offered to—"

"—talk to Denys Clifford. And so I will, when he comes here tomorrow. But I'm certainly not going to allow you to devote yourself entirely to her interests. Your job is to help me to find a house for us—for you and for me. This is the end of April. We're to be married on the first of September. That gives us four months, which may sound adequate to you, but which doesn't give us much time to find a house, perhaps wait for the vendors to get out of it, have it done up, decorate it, furnish it, choose carpets and curtains and God knows what else. Knowing you, I could guarantee that you've got those agents so confused that they're looking for white houses with a sea view within walking distance of St. James's Park."

"If I don't help her, who will?"

"Do you think that a woman with the money she's got now can't pay for all the help she needs? My father told me this evening that she's surrounded by furniture removers, shipping agents, travel agents and bank officials, all helping her."

"You said you were going to—"

"—take care of the legal side. Which I'm doing. That's one of the things my father and I discussed over dinner. But since you've lost your head, I'll relieve you of the responsibility of finding her a house. I'll undertake to find her one myself. Does that satisfy you?"

"Yes."

"Haven't you, of all people, had enough of septuagenarians? Weren't you tied for years to your grandparents, looking after them, nursing them, cooking and cleaning for them and finally burying them? After that, most people would have had enough—but you? You've adopted another one. That, in a nutshell, is what's wrong with you. You won't move forward. You won't develop. You can't or you won't understand that you're no longer stuck up in a house in a remote Yorkshire village, looking after ailing old people. You're out in the world, with equipment enough to make a place for yourself among people who matter, but you've never bothered to use it."

"All this fuss because I tried to find Lady Grantly a house."

"No. All this fuss because you didn't try to find us a house. Well, now you know. You can tell all those agents who've been advising you about houses in Portugal that you want a house here in London. You can cross Lady Grantly off your list of good works. Is that clear?"

"Loud and clear. Do you want a vase on that table?"

"No, I don't. Some fool will knock it off and ruin the carpet."

"Then I've finished, all but the clearing up."

"Do you want me to drive you home?"

"No, I don't. You can drive me to the bus, if it isn't too much trouble."

They parted with coolness. And on the following evening she arrived so late at the party that she knew he would have

further cause for annoyance; he might even think that she
had done it to annoy him.

She stood at the door on her arrival and looked round at
the guests. There was no crowd; Gerald and Claud didn't
care for crushes, so that only twenty-two people were oc-
cupying a space which would have accommodated fifty-two.
A waiter, hired for the evening, was carrying round a tray
of drinks. On tables ranged round the room were bowls of
assorted nuts, plovers' egg and mayonnaise, and heaters on
which stood miniature sausage rolls or tiny curry puffs. There
were enormous Spanish olives and tiny cheese biscuits; rolled
asparagus sandwiches that rested on crushed ice, and bread
cut into a dozen different shapes covered with anchovies or
caviar. Plenty left, she noted with satisfaction. Nobody who
came to these parties was hungry—except herself. But eating
her fill was difficult, since Gerald kept an eye on her until the
last guest had gone, by which time the waiter had removed
the food and as often as not made away with it.

Gerald was talking to Sir Denys Clifford. He came across
the room to greet her, and she reflected that at his parties
there was at least no trouble about remembering people's
names: they were framed all the way down the moving stair-
way of underground stations, they were spread across gigantic
posters all over London.

"You're late," he said, as he reached her. "Everybody's
leaving. What the devil kept you?"

She had been delayed by her involvement in one of the
frequent attacks of hysteria from which her landlady, an
ex-light-opera singer, suffered. It had been a triumph of
histrionics, but it would not have interested Gerald, or anyone else in this room.

"My watch let me down," she said. "You must buy me a nice expensive one as a wedding present."

"Come and talk to Denys—he's got a dinner date, but he waited for you. Here she is, Denys. She blames her watch, but I don't believe her."

Sir Denys looked indulgent. Recently knighted, his reputation had been built on the versatile nature of his acting, but for Emma, he forever played one part only: Gerald's father. He had the same look, the same manner, the same voice. And he liked to give advice.

"Gerald tells me," he said, "that you're looking for a house for an old lady—in Portugal."

"Yes. He said you might know of some."

"I certainly know of one. Did this friend of yours specify any particular part of the country?"

"She didn't tie me down."

"I wouldn't advise the north. Beautiful scenically, but with rather unsatisfactory summers. Chilly, to say the least. I always think it's unwise to, as it were, *plunge* into a country without finding out as much as one can. I made a point of visiting personally every place I was advised to see. That was why, in the end, I found exactly what I wanted. I must say I sold it with the greatest regret. But I've been telling Gerald —where has he got to? Ah, he's bringing you a drink. Gerald, I was just about to tell Emma about the little house close to mine, which I believe is still for sale. When I say close," he explained to Emma, "I don't of course mean cheek by jowl. The two houses are not far from one another, but they're separated by a little pine wood."

"Is there a sea view?" Emma asked.

"A charming one. There's no beach; the cliffs drop straight down to the sea, which means that there's no bathing, which means, thank Heaven, that there are no attractions for sun bathers or for picnickers. It's quite private and quite unspoilt. The house I've been speaking about—the one that might still be for sale—is a recent conversion and has never been occupied. I watched it being rebuilt, and I must say that everything was done extremely well. It's white, with very attractive shutters. Nancy Cooper—you've heard of Nancy Cooper, of course?"

"Yes."

"She was going to buy it for her parents, but when she heard that mine was for sale, she decided to buy it instead, especially as I sold it with the furniture, which of course saved her a great deal of trouble. She has, or she had, some photographs of both houses. Gerald must ask her to let you see them. I've given him the name of the lawyers in Sintra who acted for me. You should, I think, send them a telegram at once to find out whether the house is still available. And now, I'm afraid, I really must be going."

Most of the guests left with him. When the last of them had gone, and Claud had gone out too, Gerald closed the door and came to join Emma.

"What made you so late—besides a cheap watch?" he asked.

"Madam had another of her attacks."

"What caused it this time?"

"One of her pupils claimed she'd been given two lessons short. Can't you bring back some of those plates the waiter's taken away?"

"No. He's probably wrapping up everything to take home to his wife."

"I didn't eat a thing."

"Come earlier next time. Did you go and look at that house I rang you up about?"

"Yes. Terrible. The kitchen was like a cell. It would have been like being buried."

"The other rooms were all right, weren't they?"

"I didn't look. The kitchen was enough. Do you think you can get those photographs from Nancy Cooper?"

"I'll ring her up and see if she's still got them. It's amazing how your mind works."

"You're always saying it doesn't work."

"Most people would have felt that the first thing to find out was whether the house was still up for sale. What's the use of looking at photographs if it isn't?"

"Would Lady Grantly have to go out and inspect it before buying it? Sir Denys said, while you were getting me a drink, that—"

"I've heard him. Never buys without inspecting, studies a country before plunging, personal visits to every recommended site—and so on. Why do you believe everything people tell you? He happened to go out to Portugal, he saw a house, he liked it, he bought it. When the pop world threatened to move in, he moved out. All the rest was build-up."

"That makes him more like your father than ever. Are you going to ask those lawyers in Sintra whether the house is still for sale?"

"I won't put a personal call through at this moment, if that's what you mean. I'll get in touch with them tomorrow. I'll ask them, in the event of its still being on the market, to send me all the details. If they're satisfactory, and if you're sure the house is white enough, I presume I can go ahead and make a deal?"

"Yes."

"You're quite certain she authorized you to go as far as actually buying?"

"Quite sure."

"Then she's fortunate to be in the hands of people of integrity, like ourselves. You'd better write and tell her that I'm looking into this possibility—but don't make it look too hopeful. For one thing, it isn't, and for another, we don't want her rushing down here to meddle. Tell her to fold her hands and exercise patience. Has she written to you?"

"Yes."

The letters, written on paper headed *Taj Mahal Hotel, Bombay* and *The Residence, Burrapore,* had scarcely given an impression of folded hands; the picture that Emma got from them was one of Lady Grantly on the move. A letter she had received two days ago, this time headed: *Memo. Urgent: Sir Hamish Grantly,* reported progress on all fronts. The furniture was to be removed to a warehouse; three enormous containers would be required for its shipment to Portugal; there was a possibility of getting it away on a ship that would arrive at Lisbon during the first week of June.

An irate telephone call to Gerald from his father confirmed the forwardness of these preparations. They were premature, he stated, absurd, frenzied—and not one word of advice had she listened to when he took the trouble to go out and see her. The bit was between her teeth.

"Well, why not?" Emma asked, driving back with Gerald from Morning Service at Westminster Abbey. "She's got to get her furniture off, hasn't she? And once they've taken it, she'll have to get out of the house. What's so premature, absurd and frenzied about that?"

"She should have left the matter until there was definite news of a sale. She should then have left my father to deal with her house and her furniture, and gone to a quiet hotel in York until I had got all the necessary papers ready for her. I've told you before that there are rules and regulations she has to observe before she can—"

"That's your job."

"It is, and not a word of thanks will I get."

"You'll get a fee."

"I will. But if she gets herself into a mess, I'm the one who'll have to get her out of it."

"You'll get a fee for that, too. When are you going to contact the lawyers in Sintra?"

He telephoned them the following morning and rang her up.

"Oh, Gerald, is it really all right?"

"It seems so. They'll hold it until we decide. Don't get over-excited and raise her hopes yet. Just—"

"—fold my hands and exercise patience. What about the photographs?"

"I'll ring Nancy Cooper today and ask her to mail them to you."

"Do you like the sound of the house?"

"Sound? I'm satisfied with the details, if that's what you mean."

He was satisfied enough to abandon caution and agree that the property had everything that Lady Grantly needed. It was on a promontory but sheltered; it was secluded but not isolated. Sintra could be reached by car in half an hour, Lisbon in something over an hour. There was ample water, there was electricity, there was cylinder gas. The nearest village was half a mile away.

"Barring snags, it's hers," he ended. "But don't tell her until I've confirmed it. Well, are you happy now?"

She said she was, and thanked him, but she was glad that Lady Grantly had not been listening, for he made the matter —as he made the search for their own house—pure routine. A house had to be examined with a cold eye, bought or rejected, without any unnecessary prattle about atmosphere and character. That was his attitude, and it was sensible, but she thought it rather joyless. She also felt that in keeping this hopeful news from Lady Grantly she was robbing her of days of happy anticipation. There was not much fun in merely waiting.

But Lady Grantly did not wait long. She sent a telegram the next day: the furniture was to be removed, the house given up. She would leave for London on Friday. And this precipitation seemed to have spread among the lawyers, for barely had she realized the import of the telegram when Gerald telephoned. He had bought the house.

"So now you can tell her," he said. "But there's no rush to get her down here yet."

"That's what you think. She's arriving on Friday."

"What the hell for? I asked you not to say anything to her."

"So I didn't."

"If she thinks she can just take off for Portugal without delay, she's mistaken. Tell her to stay up in York."

"You tell her. Have you got the photographs?"

"No. I'll ring up Nancy Cooper and remind her."

Now was the time to tell him. He couldn't make too much fuss over the phone. She could say it quite naturally, though of course firmly: "Oh, incidentally, I've decided to go out with Lady Grantly and see her settled." Or perhaps: "I'm so glad you've got the house so quickly; that gives me time to take a quick trip out to Portugal. . . ." Or better still: "You do agree, don't you, Gerald, that it's quite impossible to let her go off on her own?" Yes, that was the one she would use.

Would have used, if he hadn't rung off.

Her lack of courage depressed her. Switching on the fire, she stood staring at it and faced for the first time the reason for her reluctance to break the news. It wasn't, she told herself hopelessly, a mere matter of his agreeing to her escorting an elderly widow to her new abode. Gerald was no fool. A girl didn't abandon her fiancé and her wedding plans at this stage unless there was a strong reason why she should do so, and he would not consider her reason strong enough. She was not related, even distantly, to Lady Grantly. She had seen her only once. She owed her no duty. However much she liked her, pitied her, wanted to protect her, her real obligation was to stay in London and proceed with the plans for her own wedding. If she didn't, her fiancé would understandably begin to wonder why she didn't. He might even go so far as to wonder whether she really wanted to marry him.

Did she? she asked herself.

Yes. At any rate, she wanted to marry. She had read countless well-reasoned arguments against marriage, but she still thought it the only sound framework for a happy home and secure, happy children. She was twenty-four, a good age to start a family, and who was there to start it with but Gerald? He wasn't exciting, but then neither was she. If the truth was that she was marrying in order to get a father for her children, was there anything wrong in that? Some might say that it was a pretty high compliment. And nobody could say that she and Gerald had rushed into this. He had taken his time, and she had been so long in making up her mind that he had shown signs of uneasiness amounting to panic.

And that was the core, the crux. He loved her. There was

condescension, patronage in his attitude towards her—but he loved her. It was a pity that she had to suppress, in his company, what he called her flippancy; it was a pity that he believed lightness of heart to be inevitably linked to lightness of head—but on a deeper level, he loved her and he would be hurt because she wanted to go to Portugal, and it would be no use telling him that for all their apparent difference in age, background and outlook, she and Lady Grantly were alike in spirit. He wouldn't understand. So she would simply tell him that she was going, and after that . . . well, after that let him say his piece.

She shook off her depression and tried to put a call through to Lady Grantly; as on previous occasions, she failed to get a reply. Doubtless the receiver was off its stand again. She sent a telegram giving as many details as she could and promising to send the photographs if she received them in time.

Lady Grantly telephoned that evening.

"Emma! It all sounds wonderful. I'm so grateful to you!"

"It was Gerald who—"

"I'm longing to see the photographs."

"If they come, I'll send them up by express mail."

"I've got all my nice things packed. I've bought quite a number of useful things—kitchen equipment and so on. And some very pretty garden chairs with canopies like little rickshaw hoods—you know the kind I mean? Have you got enough clothes for a warm climate?"

"I think so. There's a small hotel quite near here, called the Bush Hotel. Shall I book a room for you?"

"Please do. I'll arrive on Friday."

"Will you write down the address? Bush Hotel, Twelve Canberra Road."

"I'll remember."

"No, you'll forget. Get a pencil and write it down. Have you got it?"

"Yes. Canberra Hotel—"

"*Bush Hotel,* Twelve Canberra Road. Do you know what train you're coming on?"

"I can't tell you exactly. It leaves York just before tea. I shall have tea on the train. Oh, Emma, won't it be wonderful to get away from this horrid climate?"

"Yes. There's a train at three-ten, but it's a slow one."

"It may be, but the man said there wouldn't be many people travelling by it, so I chose it. You know how I hate crowds. I'm rather dreading London."

"Have you been doing too much and getting tired?"

"I'm not at all tired. How is your packing getting on?"

"I haven't begun it. There's going to be quite a lot for you to do before you can take off for Portugal. Gerald's getting the papers ready for you."

"He's been writing me letters about this and that. I do wish he'd put things more clearly. Are you sure he's a good lawyer?"

"Yes, I am. Don't lose the address of the hotel. I'll meet your train on Friday. It arrives about six-thirty at King's Cross."

"That's very kind of you, but I could easily get into a taxi and tell the man to take me to . . . Where did you say it was?"

"You wrote it down."

"So I did. On the back of this bill. I'm going to wear that little travelling suit my husband used to like so much. I always arrived looking fresh and not at all travel-stained."

"I'll be waiting for you. Six-thirty."

She put down the receiver and drew a deep breath. She

had never, she realized, really believed in any of it. It was all
very well for Lady Grantly to lay out rows of cards, pick out
a country and announce her intention of going to live there,
but other people had to keep their feet on the ground. Other
people had to remember that it was all nonsense. Nonsense
or not, out of the row of cards had emerged a new way of
life for Lady Grantly. She was going to a white house with
a sea view.

And she, Emma, was going with her. Not for long. Just to
start her off. Just to see her comfortable. Then she would
come back and search day and night for a house here in
London, and she would live in it and be a dutiful wife to
Gerald, and never leave him except for holidays in Portugal.
How wonderful to know that whenever things got too dreary
—the weather, for instance—she could get on a plane and find
herself with someone who tossed the sober facts of life up
with some cards and let them fall into new and infinitely
more exciting patterns.

She walked to the Bush Hotel and booked a room for the
following Friday; she could not say, she told them, how long
Lady Grantly would require it.

She went back to her house in a dream, so absorbed that
she all but collided with a young man who was coming down
the steps. He broke abruptly into her apology.

"You Miss Challis, by any chance?"

"Yes."

"I came to see you. Somebody said you were out, so I was
going to try again later."

He was about twenty, short and square, with a sallow skin
and a somewhat truculent air which she put down to shyness.
He spoke very fast and with a pronounced Cockney accent.

"My name's Cooper," he told her. "Len Cooper."

The mixture of confidence and expectancy in his manner told her that he thought this sufficient identification. No Len Coopers, however, sprang to her mind, and he assisted her.

"Nancy Cooper's my sister."

She looked at the bulky envelope he was carrying.

"Oh—the photographs! Thank you so much for bringing them. But you shouldn't have bothered—your sister could have mailed them."

"She was going to. Then she changed 'er mind and I said I'd take 'em because we . . . well, we . . ."

He had lost his early arrogance and was looking unhappy. He had made no move to give her the photographs.

"Matter of fact, why I came . . . Could I 'ave a word with you?" he brought out in a rush.

"Of course. Will you come in?"

She took him up to her room, puzzled but intrigued.

"Won't you sit down?"

"Thanks. Won't keep you long."

He motioned her politely to the best chair and lowered himself onto a small, spindle-legged one. He spoke at once in a tone of resolution.

"Better come out with it at once," he said.

Having decided this, he fell silent for so long that she had to prompt him.

"Come out with what?"

"With telling you why I came 'ere. But it's kind of 'ard. It sounded sensible when Nance and I talked it over, but now I'm 'ere, I can see you'll think we're . . . Well, anyway, it's this: we'd like you to do us a favour."

There was another long pause.

"What sort of favour?" she asked at last.

"Nance wanted to come 'erself, but when she goes out,

people reckernize 'er and then a crowd starts gathering and . . . Well, you know 'ow it is."

"Yes, I can understand. What's the favour?"

"I'll 'ave to explain a bit, first. Nance saw you one day when you was 'aving—"

"She came into a restaurant when I was having lunch with my fiancé, Mr. Delmont."

"That's right. She knew Mr. Delmont, or at least she'd met 'im. She didn't take to 'im. I 'ave to tell you, even if it doesn't sound polite, because it was because she didn't like 'im that Nance took such a good look at you. She thought you was a funny kind of pair. What I mean is, she wondered what sort of girl would go for a chap like 'im. And she was surprised at you being the one, because she liked the look of you. And she's a good judge, Nance is. She's young, but she's got 'er 'ead screwed on, and she can size people up. She liked you and when Mr. Delmont rang 'er up to ask if she'd send you the pictures of this 'ouse you're buying, she told me about you and we 'ad a talk and we decided to ask you this favour. And the reason I'm so long getting to the point is because I can't ask you the favour till I've told you about Dad's complaint. It was on account of 'is complaint that the doctor said 'e was to go away, go abroad. That was why Nance bought this 'ouse of Sir Denys Clifford's."

"Didn't she buy a house—"

"She bought one for Mum and Dad in Amersham. Biggest mistake she ever made. Not that there was anything wrong with the 'ouse. The 'ouse was all right. Minstrel's gallery and all that. It was the minstrel's gallery that got Nance; that, and the size of the place. It was so big, she thought she could take the crowd down there and there'd be room for 'em all— all that lot who manage 'er programs and 'er money and 'er dresses and 'er publicity. She thought she could rehearse down there, and that way, she'd see something of Mum and Dad. But it didn't work. In the first place, Mum took a look at the maids we'd got 'er, and she said if they didn't go, she would. So they went. Then Dad got this complaint and the doctor said we'd done everything too sudden. It was too much shock for 'im, living one minute in the little 'ouse in Silver Street and then all of a sudden . . . I don't suppose you've ever 'eard of Silver Street?"

"No."

"Stepney. Long row of terrace 'ouses on both sides of the street, nice and matey. We was 'appy there. Mum and Dad 'ad lived there since they got married. All their children was born there—Nance and me, and three others, older, who went to Australia a few years back. So with them gone, there was only the four of us." He paused and brooded. "We were a real family, just us four. We 'ad time to talk. We could 'ave our tea and then sit round the telly or go out and meet the . . . Well, it was a nice life. Mum and Dad often used to say we was too comfortable. Then Nance hit the jackpot and . . . well, it was like those things you read about, everybody sleeping quietly in their beds and then the dam bursts and down comes the water and drowns 'em all. Nance could take it. I could take it. But Mum and Dad couldn't."

Once again he paused, his brown eyes full of trouble. Emma did not speak.

"We got Mum and Dad to retire. We folded up Mum's aprons and floor cloths and polishing rags and made a bonfire of 'em. That's 'ow crazy we were. We got 'em out of Silver Street and told 'em they were going to live 'appy ever after, with Nance making so much dough, we'd stopped counting it, and me doing all right as a song writer. We put 'em in this 'ouse at Amersham, and then Dad's complaint came on."

"I'm sorry. What did he—"

"It was the shock. The doctor said we shouldn't never 'ave taken Dad out of 'is proper sphere. We 'adn't considered the psychological repercussions, was what 'e called it. What it came to in plain language was that Nance and me between us, 'ad made a muck of it. And I can't even say that we did it for Mum and Dad's sake, because part of it was we was afraid of what people would say if Nance and I got rich and moved out and left our old parents stewing in Silver Street, see? They couldn't go back, because the 'ouse got passed to the next on the list, and anyway, the doctor said that Dad 'ad to be got right away to some place that'd be new and strange, and take 'is mind off. A foreign country, 'e said. So that's why Nance bought this 'ouse in Portugal. Mum said she'd go for Dad's sake, but we could see she was dreading it. I flew out with 'em and left 'em there. I got back yesterday, and Nance was waiting to tell me about you and ask me to come and see you to ask you this favour. And this is what the favour is: Will you go and pay Mum a visit now and then?"

Emma looked at him. "I don't think you understand," she said. "The house next to your mother's isn't being bought for us. It's for an old lady called Lady Grantly, who's going to live out in Portugal and—"

She stopped. The disappointment in his eyes was more than she could bear. She hurried on.

"—and I shall only be out there a little while, just to settle her in, but I shall certainly—"

"You're going with 'er?"

"Yes."

"Would you go and see Mum?"

"Of course I will. I'll take Lady Grantly, too. Your mother couldn't have a nicer, kinder person as a neighbour. If you hadn't come to ask me a favour, I should have gone across to ask your mother a favour: to keep an eye on Lady Grantly. She'll be there all alone, and she isn't . . . she needs someone to keep . . . it's hard to explain, but I promise you that she'll need your mother as much as your mother will need her. As soon as I get out there, I'll take Lady Grantly across to see your mother, and I'm prepared to bet that the two of them will become good friends."

He said nothing for a time. Then he got up and went to stare out of the window. "Poor old Dad," he said huskily to the chimney pots opposite. "Poor bloody old Dad. 'Appy as a sandboy all 'is life, not a day off for sickness, all his pals at the local, bingo just down the road, and we take 'im away from it all and . . ."

"I've promised, haven't I?" Emma asked.

He turned. "Yes. Thanks. And what I 'aven't said is that Nance and I wouldn't 'ave asked anybody else to do this. It was just that she saw you and thought you 'ad a friendly look. But remember one thing." He pushed a chair out of the way with his foot and walked to the door. "Mum's no cadger. She's the independent sort. She won't make the first move. If you don't go to see 'er, she won't go to see you. See what I mean?"

"Yes. I'm only sorry I'm not going to be out there longer."

"It'll be long enough, if you can get the two old girls together. It sounds a funny mixture, my mum and Lady Somebody, but when you see Mum, you'll see there isn't all that difference. And all she needs is someone she can go to if Dad's complaint gets 'er down. I'd like to go out there and keep an eye on 'im, but Mum won't 'ear of it; she wants me over 'ere, keeping watch on Nance in case she gets to smoking pot or sleeping with the announcers. Well, thanks, Miss Challis. Don't come down. I'm not afraid of the old battle-axe who let me in before. Foreigner, is she?"

"Italian. She used to be an opera singer. She gives singing lessons."

"Not Nance's kind of singing, I bet."

"Just a moment," Emma said, as he was turning away. "Did you say you'd taken your mother and father out to Portugal?"

"Yes."

"Did you see the house your sister nearly bought—the smaller one Lady Grantly's going to?"

"Cor! Nearly forgot." He plunged a hand into a pocket. "Snaps," he said, bringing them out and handing them to Emma. "Took 'em when I was out there. Nance said you'd like to see 'em."

Emma took them. They were in colour, and showed two white houses and the gardens that surrounded them.

"That's the one Mum and Dad's in. That other's yours. You can keep 'em if you like." He picked up the larger envelope from the table on which he had placed it, and slipped the photographs out of it. "You can see the coastline in these. And the pine wood that's in between the two 'ouses."

"It all looks heavenly," Emma said with feeling. "Surely your mother's going to be happy out there."

"Depends 'ow Dad's complaint goes." He held out a hand. "Goodbye, Miss Challis. And thanks. And if you ever want any tickets for any of Nance's shows . . . but I don't suppose you like that sort, do you?"

"I'll go straight out tomorrow and buy some of her records."

For the first time, he laughed, and looked like the carefree boy he must have been in Silver Street.

"Save your dough. She'll send you some," he said.

The door closed behind him, and she sat down to examine the photographs. She looked at them for a long time, and then she put them with the snaps into the envelope and addressed it to Lady Grantly. She clipped to the photographs a card on which she had written, as an extra precaution, the name and address of the Bush Hotel. Then she went to the post office.

But as she came back to the house, she was not thinking of Lady Grantly or of the house in Portugal. She was wondering what Mr. Cooper's complaint could be.

Chapter
4

She borrowed Gerald's car to meet Lady Grantly at the station and got there in good time for the train. For once, she was glad to feel the chill of the vast, gloomy interior, for the cold weather, so long in departing, had given way at last to a burst of unseasonable heat. Perspiring commuters were carrying their coats and unbuttoning their jackets. Bus conductors sweated in their heavy uniforms. Shopkeepers unrolled sunblinds. In the parks, crowds seemed to have sprung up in colourful clumps on the grass, while in deck chairs, the elderly basked under the shelter of newspapers. Winter was over, spring had been skipped, summer was here.

The train came in. Emma, waiting at the barrier, watched the passengers as they began to drift past her. The stream thinned and dried up, but there was no sign of Lady Grantly.

A group of porters standing near one of the carriages afforded a few moments of hope—they might be preparing to deal with what Lady Grantly called hand luggage. But they proved to be merely chatting; they dispersed and the ticket collector prepared to close the gates.

"Could I go and look in the carriages?" Emma asked him. "I'm expecting an old lady."

"Think she might have fallen asleep?"

"She may have."

"Well if she has, you'd better wake her up, or she'll find herself going back to where she came from."

She walked the length of the train—nobody. She went to the arrivals board, found that another train from the north would be in at seven, and waited for it. It duly arrived, but Lady Grantly was not on it. Emma decided to find out if she had arrived on an earlier train and gone to the hotel.

Lady Grantly? No, not so far; had she cancelled?

"No. Keep the room, please. She's delayed."

She went out to the car and drove home. Lady Grantly had not been there. She drove back to the hotel—still no sign.

She stopped on her way out and looked in perplexity at the hall porter. "This *is* number twelve Canberra Road, isn't it?"

"That's right, miss. Number twelve. Why? Think the lady might have made a mistake?"

"She shouldn't have; I told her it was the Bush Hotel. Well, I'll go back to the station."

She was in the car when he came down the steps and called to her. "Just a minute, miss. I've just thought of something. There's another Canberra Road, you know."

"Oh, is there?" Emma felt a surge of relief. "That may explain it. Can you tell me where it is?"

"Out Notting Hill way. Leave the underground on your left. It's a turning off Jervis Avenue, if I remember right."

"Thank you."

She drove to Notting Hill and found that it had improved

out of all recognition since she had walked round the district on her arrival in London, looking for somewhere inexpensive to live. There were new, smart apartments and wide streets— but Jervis Avenue had not come within the circle made by the planners' pencil. Unkempt, neglected, it straggled dispiritedly northward, spawning weedy offspring as it went. One of these proved to be Canberra Road, with two lines of shabby houses, the shabbiest of which was number twelve. The district seemed to be populated entirely by West Indians who had done their best to relieve the prevailing greyness and gloom by splashing vivid paint on doors and windows.

There were stone steps leading up to the front door of number twelve, but Emma's passage was obstructed by several young men and girls who were sitting outside to enjoy the warmth of the evening. They made way for her, and she mounted the steps and paused at the open door.

"You goes right in, dear," one of the girls told her lazily. "Open house."

It was, indeed. Emma, taking a step into the hall, saw round her four more open doors, each giving a free view of the activities being pursued by the people inside the rooms. In one, a large, turbaned woman was ironing clothes and singing at the top of her voice. In the room opposite, a man sat at a cobbler's last, mending boots. But it was the room on her left that Emma approached, since it was clearly the one which served as an office.

It also served as a bedroom and a dining room. In a far corner was a large and lumpy-looking double bed; next to it was a wardrobe painted yellow, and beyond that a small square table laid for two. A gas ring and a sink were in a corner. Close to the door was a dressing table littered with powder, pins, jars, bottles and a pile of letters and papers.

Hanging outside the door was a large notice which bore threats secured by drawing pins:

Joey, you bang doors after three in the morning, you get what's coming to you.

Hey Martha, if you going make fried onions, you don't stink up the landing no more, see?

Jinny, you take youse stiletto heels off coming down these stairs, or else.

And more ominously:

Abigail, you still owing.

The room was occupied; a young woman, her back to the door, was standing looking into a wall mirror near the sink, putting rollers into her hair. She glimpsed Emma and turned, her mouth full of long and lethal-looking pins.

"Hm?" She emptied the pins into her hand and took a second surprised look. "You ain't come after rooms, have you?"

Emma shook her head. "No. I—"

"Wait a lil minute, jes' let me get this last sausage done up." She rolled up the last strand of hair, stuck pins in with alarming speed and recklessness, and then came to lean on the door. "Now tell me, dear. You lost your way?"

"No. But I think an old lady I'm looking for might have—"

"—come here? White lady? Black lady? Brown lady? Yellow lady?"

"White lady."

"Well, I ain't seen no white lady here, but then, I've jes' come in. Hey, Gabriel!" she screamed. "Gabriel!"

A figure appeared—a lanky black youth who hung dangerously over the banisters.

"Calling me, Myrtle?"

"When you sat in this office taking care for me, did any old lady show up?"

"Yeah. One."

"How many you expect?" shrilled Myrtle. "What she say when she come?"

Gabriel, with an easy, graceful movement, swung a leg over the banisters and came sliding down them with a velocity that took him right through the hall and out of the front door.

"Ha, clever! You see?" screamed Myrtle. "One day you land upside down on your head, and praise the Lawd for that. What this lady say?"

Gabriel, returning and seating himself on the bottom stair, informed her that the old lady had asked if her room was ready.

"Her *what?*" Myrtle's voice cracked under the strain. "What's this room? Where's this room?"

"That's what I asked her. I said, 'What's this room?' She said it had been ordered for sure. So I said, 'Well, I don't know nothing about no room for a lady like you, but I'm not the boss man, so what you do, you wait till Myrtle comes, and she'll fix it.' "

"Then if you said wait, where's she, eh? Where you put her?" Myrtle demanded.

"I got a chair—that one." He pointed to the wooden chair in front of the dressing table. "I put it in the hall and she sat on it and I went back to my—what-you-say—duties, and bye'n by I ask her: 'That a taxi you got outside?' and she says, 'Yes-oh-my-goodness-me-I-plumb-forgot-that's-my-luggage.' "

"Luggage? Where's this luggage?" Myrtle gazed wildly round the hall.

"I'm telling you, Myrt, I'm *telling* you."

"Why didn't you tell me when I came home, eh?"

"Because you brought that Mimi Sylvester with you, and you know what she—"

"Yes, yes, yes, I know. She chased you up the stairs, and nobody's seen her from that time since. So where's this old lady?"

"She was going out to talk to this taxi driver, and Joey's sitting on the steps, and he gets up and goes with her to help her, and they ask the taxi driver to wait some more, and then they get to talking, and next thing he says he's from Barbados and she says, 'Well, ain't that the ways of Providence, I'm from Barbados myself,' and they shakes hands, and she pats his shoulder and he starts crying, right out loud out there, and next thing they get into the taxi with the luggage and Joey shouts to me that they'll be back."

"And they ain't back, so what?" Myrtle asked distractedly. "What you think Joey doing, taking her off like that with the taxi and the luggage?"

This question, which nobody could have answered, proved unnecessary. From outside came the throb of a taxi's engine. Emma, pushed to the door by a Myrtle anxious not to miss a thing, saw a large, middle-aged West Indian assisting Lady Grantly to alight.

"Emma—my dear Emma! We came back to fetch you!"

Emma took a deep breath. She had been looking forward to this meeting, but she had not realized how much she had wanted to hear that high, fluting voice again.

She went down the steps. Lady Grantly was dressed in a dun-coloured suit which had a matching, jaunty little cloak; she was wearing low-heeled shoes and a pork-pie hat. She looked well-groomed, even fashionable; that it was the fashion of forty years ago did not seem to matter.

She kissed Emma affectionately. "This was the wrong place, but what do you think? This gentleman comes from Barbados."

Emma held out a hand and it disappeared into a large black one. Joey had stopped crying and was wearing a wide, delighted grin.

"Took the lady to the right address," he told Emma. "You see how it is, I know this other Canberra Road. One time I drove a van, and I delivered right at the Bush Hotel."

"We found it, and my room was ready, and I left my luggage there and Joey said we must come back, because the hall porter said you had gone off to the wrong place, you silly little thing. What would have happened if Joey hadn't known about this other address, I can't imagine! I should never have found you!"

Their departure was relatively quiet. Myrtle, after one glance at the pork-pie hat, had been struck dumb. Gabriel was standing with his mouth open in an effort to work out which address was which. The group seated on the steps attempted to console Joey, who was crying again.

The taxi was paid for. Emma put Lady Grantly into Gerald's car and had to wait while she leaned out to express a warm invitation to Joey to drop in next time he was passing Portugal. Then she leaned back and gave a sigh of contentment.

"So lovely to see you again, Emma. I *missed* you. That's why I was so anxious to get everything packed up, so that I could come here and enjoy your company again. Now you must tell me everything from the beginning. I've been reading about Portugal—I do believe, don't you, in getting to know all one can about a place one's going to live in? I'd got it quite in the wrong place, too low down on the map, but I've got it right now. I've also been listening to some language records I bought—what are they called?"

"Linguaphone?"

"Yes. You listen, and you follow it all in a little book. I find I can't listen and follow at the same time, but I daresay I shall learn in time. Now tell me, do you really like my house?"

"It looks lovely. Gerald says you've got a good building on a first-class site. He's got a nice pile of papers ready for you to sign."

"His father has been most interfering lately; I was so glad to see the last of him. You won't have to go out to work any more now that I'm here, will you?"

"I should, but I won't."

"I shall pay you a handsome salary for looking after me. Did you remember to ask those lawyers in Portugal to arrange a nice car for us? I've got such wonderful plans, Emma; we're going to enjoy living out there. Aren't you excited?"

Emma said that she was and wondered who had written the lines about the tangled web woven by deceivers. Not only had she to tell Gerald she was going to Portugal; she had to convince Lady Grantly that she was not going to stay there.

They reached the Bush Hotel and found a message at the desk: Mr. Delmont had telephoned and would be pleased if Lady Grantly and Miss Challis would dine with him.

"No," said Lady Grantly. "You see, Emma? I knew he wouldn't stop at arranging my affairs. Now he's trying to be friendly."

"You don't know the first thing about what he's been doing

for you," Emma pointed out. "He's got to talk to you—why shouldn't it be over dinner? Unless you're feeling tired."

"I'm not at all tired. What have I done but sit quietly in a train? If you think I should get this over with, then I will, but I would much rather have had a nice little meal somewhere with you."

"I'll go home and change and ring him up from there. Would eight-thirty suit you?"

"It would suit me very well. That gives me time to have a nice hot bath."

Emma was back at the hotel at a quarter past eight. She sent a message up to Lady Grantly and then went to sit in a small and cheerless lounge in which two very old gentlemen were reading. She hoped they were deaf; this was the moment she had chosen to tell Gerald that she was going to Portugal. If she postponed the revelation any longer, Lady Grantly would forestall her by making some reference to the fact during dinner. Now was the time and the place; he could hardly make too much of a scene here.

He began by making a mild one on his arrival, when he discovered that the hotel had no license and that he could get nothing to drink.

"If you'd told me," he told Emma, "I could have arranged to meet somewhere else. How long's she going to be, do you think? It's half past."

"Not quite. She won't be long. And there's something I want to say to you before she comes. It's about—"

"If it's about the house I asked you to look at, that's just what I was going to ask you. Did you go and see it?"

"Yes."

"What's it like?"

"Not bad. I'll tell you about it later. I just want—"

"That's the first time you've gone as far as admitting that something was reasonably decent. You've actually found a kitchen that suits you?"

"Yes. Listen, Gerald—"

"What's the view like?"

"Bad. You look across the road to two shops."

"What's at the back?"

"The backs of other houses."

"Garden?"

"Very small. Made into a kind of courtyard with a little round pool in the middle. Arty, but rather clever. Look, Gerald, there's something—"

She stopped. Lady Grantly had unfortunately chosen this occasion on which to be punctual. She was at the door, and Gerald had risen. And though Emma had often been irritated by his tendency to pay too much attention to the stares of strangers, she felt some sympathy for him as she saw what Lady Grantly was wearing: a rather long black dress, a short coat of gold stuff, a watch fastened to a chain and attached to her bosom, and a large black beaded cummerbund. She knew Gerald was praying that they would not encounter any of his friends on the way to the restaurant, but she was interested to observe the look of wistful admiration in the eyes of the two old gentlemen.

"Your car keys." She handed them to Gerald. "Thanks for the loan of the car."

Dinner went without a hitch for the simple reason that both Gerald and Lady Grantly were determined to talk business only. She wanted details and he was anxious to supply them. Between courses he showed her documents and papers; during courses he outlined anything else she wanted to know. At any indication that she was about to stray from essentials, Emma led her gently back. If Gerald noticed her unvarying use of *we* as opposed to *I*, he gave no sign. By the time they had ordered coffee, he looked exhausted but relieved; she had seen and approved of the photographs, she had agreed that the price was reasonable, and she had promised to sign all the other documents that he had handed over to Emma. As far as he was concerned, she was all but on her way, no longer a threat to his father's peace of mind or to his own.

"That's the lot for the moment, I think," he said, and signalled the waiter to bring the bill. "I've written to the lawyers out there and given them instructions about the car and the maids and so on. The office is in Sintra, as you know, not in Lisbon. It's run by a Portuguese named Melo, but I've been dealing with an English associate of his called Weybridge. I'm glad I was able to find a house for you. Emma hadn't been very successful in producing anything, so I took matters into my own hands. That left her free to look for houses in London. I've decided that buying is more satisfactory than renting."

"I think so, too. But won't you find running a house rather a trouble?" Lady Grantly asked.

"I think you've forgotten—I told you I was going to be married."

"So you did. I hope my memory isn't going. I must thank you for the arrangements you've made for me. I hope you succeeded in finding something equally satisfactory for yourself."

"Emma's doing that."

"Well, she must hurry up."

"That's what I've been telling her. But I'm afraid her mind has been more on Portugal than on London lately."

"Can you wonder? Can you blame her if, like me, she's a little excited? Neither of us has ever been there."

Gerald stared at her. "Been where?"

"Portugal, of course. Weren't we talking about Portugal?"

"You're not expecting Emma to go out there with you, I hope?"

His eyes went to Emma, but hers were on her clasped hands; she was practising a feat at which her grandmother had been expert—wafting herself away in spirit and returning only when the awkward moment had passed.

"You didn't expect me to go out there alone, did you?" Lady Grantly asked in surprise.

"Frankly, I did. And do," Gerald told her. "Emma has no time to go out to Portugal, or anywhere else. She's looking for a house, and when she's found it, there's going to be a lot to do to it before it's ready to move into. Perhaps you don't know that the marriage is to be in September?"

There was a faint sneer in the words that was not lost on Lady Grantly. A patch of red appeared on each of her cheeks. Emma read the signs with dismay. Anger, she knew, would only lead to confusion.

"I'm not in touch with any of your plans," Lady Grantly informed Gerald. "Especially plans for your marriage."

"Our marriage."

"Well, naturally, when people speak of a marriage, they must speak in the plural. It takes two, everybody knows that. All I want to know is how you can imagine that this affects Emma?"

He addressed Emma. "Will you kindly make it clear to Lady Grantly that you and I are to be married in September, and that you are quite unable to agree to this absurd plan to go out to Portugal, for however short a time? I would have said—"

"You mean marry *Emma?*" Lady Grantly broke in. "Is *that* what you mean? Emma, you must disabuse him at once. He must understand that—"

"I wonder," Gerald asked her, white with rage and embarrassment, "if you'd be so good as to keep your voice down?"

"Do you deny," Lady Grantly asked him in the same clear tones, "that when you came to see me—unasked, I may say— up in Yorkshire, you informed me that you were engaged?"

"Certainly I did. I—"

"I'm thankful you at least have the grace to admit it. I remember distinctly sending a message of warning to your fiancée. How do you explain *that* incident, may I ask?"

"All this," he told her, "has nothing whatsoever to do with you."

"No? Really, you can't have been paying attention to what we talked about during dinner. This whole plan, the plan you've held forward by arranging the purchase of this house, is to do with me. You have bought it for *me*. It is *I* who will occupy it. *I* am going to Portugal. It is with *me* that Emma is going. So isn't it a little extraordinary to say that I have nothing to do with it?"

"Emma," Gerald said loudly and distinctly, "is not going to Portugal, with you or with anybody else. Emma is going to stay here and marry me. Emma, will you kindly corroborate that?"

"No. Yes. The fact is," Emma said, "that I ought to have made it clear that I think it's impossible for Lady Grantly to—"

"Lady Grantly," Gerald broke in, "has lived a good many

years in a good many countries without any help from you. She is perfectly capable of taking herself to Portugal and settling herself into her house. If she isn't, she can afford to find people who will assist her. She has no claim whatsoever on you. If you think that an acquaintance so slight justifies your taking this absurdly protective attitude, I think it's time you realized that you are behaving idiotically. May we now end this discussion? If you've finished your coffee . . ."

"I haven't, and I am not going to be hurried," Lady Grantly said firmly. "You have spoken of protective attitudes. I shall now take up one towards Emma. I may have no claim on her, but she has one on me. I will not stand by and watch a charming young girl be taken in. It is monstrous that you should go about claiming a fiancée in Yorkshire and another in London and—who knows?—another somewhere else."

The diners surrounding them had given up all pretense of eating, but by now Gerald was past caring.

"I'm not going to attempt to argue with you," he said. "It would be a waste of time."

"*And* breath," agreed Lady Grantly. "I haven't forgotten how you deserted your father when you should have stood by him and prevented him from making a—"

"This is your fault," he said bitterly to Emma. "You must have known this was going to come up. You could at least have made your position clear."

"*I* have made the position clear," Lady Grantly told him. "I am going to keep a motherly, a grandmotherly eye on her. She is a girl whose kind heart leads her astray, and you have taken advantage of her. I shall certainly take her to Portugal with me, and then you can get your matrimonial plans straightened out. They do not interest me."

Gerald had paid the bill. They rose, and he followed them out to the street.

"Will you kindly get me a taxi?" Lady Grantly asked him. "Emma, will you come with me?"

Emma looked from her to Gerald. They were both seething with fury, but she thought that Gerald's blood pressure would probably stand it better than Lady Grantly's.

"Yes," she said. "Thank you for the dinner, Gerald."

They left him standing on the pavement. But when Emma had seen Lady Grantly safely into the hotel and gone back to her house, his car was outside and he was standing beside it. He paid the taxi, watched it out of sight and then wasted no words.

"Will you admit now that she's completely off her head?"

"Isn't that an added reason for not letting her go out there alone?"

"What gets me is that it isn't only protective. You . . . you actually *like* her. That's what makes the whole thing so hard to understand."

"Perhaps it's my early training in looking after old people."

"Your grandparents were sane. She isn't."

"Yes, she is."

"You seriously mean to tell me that you intend to go out there with her? You're going to leave me, leave our plans in the air, leave everything to do with our wedding . . . And for how long, for God's sake?"

"That's up to you. If you'll see that the lawyers over there hurry up and engage servants for her, all I'll have to do is help her to arrange the furniture and then come home again."

He turned to study her expression under the street lamp, and something in his face moved her.

"I'm sorry I didn't tell you before, Gerald. That's what I

was just beginning to say in the hotel tonight, when she came in and—"

"When did you make up your mind?"

"That first day up in Yorkshire. I couldn't bear to think of her getting . . . getting lost. You said yourself she was more peculiar now than she used to be. It didn't matter how peculiar she was while she was living in a little house with nothing more dangerous to do than take the bus into York and back. But this trip to Portugal was something else. I couldn't imagine how she could do it by herself. You said she was rich, and so people would help her; that's true, but they'd be, as often as not, the types that would help themselves, too. I'm sorry. I'm sorry I didn't tell you and I'm sorry I've been so long finding us a house, but if you find one you like while I'm away, you can go ahead and buy it and I promise to like it."

"How about setting a definite time limit to this little jaunt?"

"I will if you like. I forgot to mention that she was paying all my expenses. But as I don't yet know when we're going, I can hardly fix a date for coming back, can I?"

He did not answer in words. Taking a step forward, he pulled her close and kissed her, and she realized that the exchange with Lady Grantly had roused more than his temper.

"Emma, look . . ." He was speaking in a tone she had never heard him use. "You and I—"

A light snapped on in the house, throwing a circle of brightness round them.

"Hell and damnation," he swore slowly.

He had retreated, and Emma was not sorry. Getting out her latchkey and letting herself into the house, she realized that she had had enough for one day.

Chapter
5

Lady Grantly had been advised by both Gerald and his father to go out to Portugal by sea; perhaps for this reason she elected to go by train. She and Emma took the train ferry to Paris, and there caught the Sud Express. As soon as they had left Paris behind, she led Emma to the restaurant car, where they had lunch, Lady Grantly remarking on the smoothness and silence of their passage, so pleasant after the clanking of chains that had disturbed her during the Channel crossing. Emma found her claim to speak French amply justified, and hoped that her own Spanish, when she came to use it, would prove as fluent.

They changed at Irun from the French to the Spanish line, and most of the available porters were required to transfer Lady Grantly's hide suitcases, her bags and baskets, books and rugs to her sleeping compartment. Emma saw her installed and then said good night.

She went to breakfast next morning in the restaurant car and sent coffee and rolls in to Lady Grantly. At midday she saw her come into the corridor, once more wearing her dun-coloured outfit. She was not so well pleased with this train, which was proceeding at what she called a slow trot. Emma, enjoying every moment, pointed out that they were now in a country in which time was not of much account. With a map and a guide book, she was following the route. The only shadow over her happiness was the memory of her parting with Gerald who, as the time for her departure grew nearer, had grown progressively more morose. A wide crack had appeared in his sophistication, leaving his feeling of insecurity exposed. Even the fact that they had at last found a suitable house could not cheer him.

"You'll come back soon, Emma?"

"Of course. Haven't I told you?"

"Suppose you change your mind when you get out there?"

"Why should I?"

"You might get involved in something or other."

"There won't be time."

"Three weeks. You won't go back on that?"

"No."

That was time enough, she estimated. Everything so far had gone without a hitch, and she had been very much impressed by the efficient link-up between those who wanted something and those who, a thousand miles away, were willing to supply it. The house, a car, two maids, a chauffeur; someone to see the furniture through the Customs, someone to transfer it to the house; the garden to be tidied up, electricity to be switched on, gas cylinders ordered. All Lady Grantly had had to do was pay—and pay. Emma had known the power of money, but this was the first time she had seen it demonstrated.

The second night of the journey was almost as comfortable

as the first. The next morning came the halt at the frontier town of Vilar Formosa—blue tiles on the station buildings, and Portuguese officials who looked darker and more melancholy than their Spanish neighbours.

"Portugal," Lady Grantly said with satisfaction. "I've enjoyed the journey."

"It isn't over yet. Several more hours."

Hours of unbroken sunshine and increasing heat. It was only the third week of May, but Emma was already realizing that what she had thought cool dresses were not going to be nearly cool enough.

The train puffed and sighed its way up to Guarda—three thousand feet above sea level, she read aloud from her guide book. After Guarda, sheep country—great open uplands where the gay striped blankets were dyed, the dyeing done not in factories but in the fields, near the wells, with hanks of bright blue and green and red yarn hung over stone walls. The—

There was no point in continuing; Lady Grantly had fallen asleep. She woke up for lunch—a Portuguese meal of vegetable soup, boiled fish, thick and not-too-tasty steaks and little round caramel custards. Then Emma went back to her map. The train ran so close to the river Tagus that at some points it seemed possible to lean out and touch the women working on little patches of land between tiny riverside shacks. This part of the country, said the guide book, was frequently flooded in winter. Emma wondered what happened to the women in the shacks.

Santarem. The home stretch. Lady Grantly began to collect the books, the knitting, the boiled sweets, the paper tissues, the comfortable slippers, the sun glasses, the bottled mineral water and the fruit that had contributed to her ease throughout the journey. There had been no disorder in her compartment; everything had been given a place, everything had been kept in its place. It was only Lady Grantly's mind that was untidy.

She stepped down onto the platform on their arrival and looked round her with undisguised delight.

"Lisbon! Lovely! And warm! Just look at that lovely sunshine outside, Emma, and the policeman with a white topee, just like India. And *armies* of porters!"

From the armies, Emma selected two. Her Spanish, she had already discovered, was understood by the Portuguese. What they said to her in reply was unfortunately not so clear, but she was beginning to pick out words which were similar in both languages.

At the ticket barrier, they were approached by a young, thin-faced chauffeur who handed Lady Grantly a letter. She read its few lines.

"He's ours," she told Emma. "His name is Alípio. Good afternoon, Alípio."

Alípio, cap in hand, bowed and substantiated the letter's claim to his knowledge of English.

"Good afternoon, madame. Good afternoon, miss. We go to the hotel now, if you agree to this."

"Can you fit all the luggage?" Emma asked.

He glanced at it. "No, miss. Some will follow in taxi."

They went in convoy to the taxi line—Alípio, Lady Grantly and Emma, the two laden porters. Their hotel, on the Avenida da Liberdade, was comfortable and it was also quiet until Lady Grantly opened the window of her bedroom and let in the rattle of the trams that were going past.

"If you like," Emma offered, "I'll take this room and you can have mine—it faces a side street."

"I shall *enjoy* the noise," said Lady Grantly. "And I shall enjoy watching all the people going past. Not a beautiful race, I wouldn't say. Lovely children, but then they seem to go off. Are you going to telephone to somebody?"

"Yes. Room service, for tea. You said you were dying."

"So I was, so I am. Do you think they call tea *Cha* because the Portuguese learnt it in India, or do you think the Indians picked it up from the Portuguese? I think I'm going to pick this language up very quickly. You must help me once we get settled."

"Once *you* get settled." Emma made the correction mechanically. It had, as usual, no effect whatsoever.

"When are we going to see the house?" Lady Grantly asked. "Alípio said that Mr.—what was that lawyer's name?"

"Weybridge."

"Well, he was going to telephone."

The call came half an hour later, when Lady Grantly was in her bath. On the line was not Mr. Weybridge but a girl who spoke good English and who said that she was his secretary.

"Can you give me a message?" Emma asked her. "Lady Grantly isn't available at the moment."

"Certainly. Mr. Weybridge would be pleased if you would come to this office tomorrow morning, if this is convenient. The chauffeur knows where it is. Would you prefer eleven, or half-past eleven?"

"Eleven," Emma decided. "That gives us more time to see the house."

"I am sorry Senhor Melo is not here to see you—he is away in Madeira. But it is Mr. Weybridge who has made all the arrangements. Will you please remind Lady Grantly that she

will need her passport and all the papers which were sent to
Mr. Delmont in England?"

"I will."

"Thank you. That is all. Goodbye."

Efficient, Emma thought. Nice and crisp and no waste of
words. Someone who would perhaps be able to deal with
Lady Grantly's tendency to go off the point.

The morning was bright and sunny, and Alípio was waiting
for them when they went downstairs. His duties seemed to
include his services as guide, for as they drove to Sintra, he
pointed out to them everything he thought might be of
interest. He turned away from the busy shopping district of
Sintra and drove past the municipal buildings and the park to
the square in front of the palace. In one of the nearby buildings was Senhor Melo's office, with his name and profession
painted in highly decorative lettering on the wall.

They were received by a small, slight girl with eyes even
larger and more lustrous than Alípio's. Her glossy black hair
was drawn back and tied at the neck with a neat scarlet bow.

"Come in, please. Mr. Weybridge will see you in a few
minutes. Will you please wait in here?"

Waiting was no hardship. The room into which she showed
them was lined with shelves, and ranged along them were
pairs of miniature footwear of every colour, every period and
every style. No pair was more than an inch in length, but the
details were perfect. There were sabots, spurred military
boots, Chinese slippers, football boots, dancing pumps, high-
button boots, snow shoes, climbers' boots, elegant eighteenth-
century shoes and clumsy Cromwellian ones. Fascinated,
Lady Grantly and Emma walked round inspecting them, so
absorbed that only the sudden increase of brightness in the
room made Emma realize that the door was open and a man

was standing on the threshold. On either side of him was a beautiful Great Dane, and her first thought, as she took in the group, was that she was looking at three magnificent animals.

It must be Senhor Melo, she decided, though the secretary had said he was away. This man was too dark to be an Englishman. On the other hand, he was taller, broader and more powerful-looking than any Portuguese she had yet seen. Then she heard him speak.

"Lady Grantly? I'm Robert Weybridge. Welcome to Portugal."

"Mr. Weybridge!" Lady Grantly shook hands warmly. "What beautiful, beautiful dogs—are they yours?"

"Yes. They're feeling the heat a bit. I shouldn't have brought them into Sintra."

"This is Miss Challis, who has very kindly come to stay with me."

Mr. Weybridge bowed, confirming the un-English impression Emma had received. Like most large men, his movements were deliberate, but he had in addition a leisurely air that she thought bordered on laziness. He had fine brown eyes, broad cheekbones and a firm jaw.

"I see you're admiring Senhor Melo's collection," he said. "He's very proud of it. Every pair is quite authentic, as you've probably discovered. He went to a great deal of trouble to get the details correct. These, for example." He took two slow strides and picked up a tiny pair of Roman sandals. "He had them made of untanned hide. They were called *carbatina*. They were worn by Roman citizens but not by slaves." He replaced them, arranging their leather thongs carefully, and picked up another pair. "About the year fifteen hundred. Elegant, but I can't imagine how men could have got about in them. My favourites are these little button boots. High heels and pearl buttons—do you see?"

"So tiny, yet so perfect," Lady Grantly said. "What's that little scarlet pair up there?"

He got them down for her. Emma looked and admired, but she was beginning to feel impatient. They were here not to admire Senhor Melo's collection of footwear but to sign papers and see a house. To her relief, the secretary appeared in the doorway.

"The papers are ready for you, Mr. Weybridge."

"Thanks, Milou. We're coming."

But he showed them three more pairs of shoes first. Then, ordering the dogs out of the way, he led them across a corridor and into a room with a large desk on which were neat stacks of documents. Milou pushed a chair forward for Lady Grantly and placed beside it a small table. Mr. Weybridge put Emma in a tall-backed chair of Spanish design and then installed himself in the swivel chair behind his desk.

Thereafter, it seemed to Emma, he took very little interest in the proceedings. Milou spread papers before Lady Grantly and explained their import; from time to time she asked Mr. Weybridge's opinion on a legal point, and he gave it. When the legal matters were at an end and the domestic side of the arrangements were explained, he gave up all pretense of interest; he adjusted the collar of one of the dogs, stared absently out of the window and twice glanced at his watch.

"Two maids have been engaged for you," Milou told Lady Grantly.

"Good. What are their names?"

"The older one is called Gracinda. She is about thirty. The other one is Lourdes; she is only sixteen, but she is a good worker. Both of them are from the village, Aldeia da Torre."

"Does the chauffeur come from there, too?"

"No. His village is halfway between Aldeia da Torre and Sintra. He will go on a bicycle to your house every day."

"Is he a chauffeur pure and simple, or will he work in the garden if he's asked to?" Lady Grantly enquired.

"You have a gardener already. The chauffeur works only with the car."

"And you'd better know," Mr. Weybridge put in, "that he is neither pure nor simple. But he drives well and he'll look after your car."

"About your furniture," Milou went on. "I have got all the details here—when it was shipped from England, when it will arrive. I will arrange to send somebody to the docks. Will you be staying in Lisbon until it comes, or do you intend to move to Sintra?"

"We'll stay in Lisbon and go sight-seeing," Lady Grantly decided. "Which direction is the house in, Mr. Weybridge?"

He got up, opened a window and pointed. "You can't see very clearly today; there's a slight mist. If you follow that little military plane that's flying up there, you'll see more or less where the village is. You know, of course"—he closed the window and went back to the desk—"that your house is a conversion? You're fortunate, I think, to get something so strongly constructed. And the alterations were done by a very good builder."

"Who owned the house?" Emma asked.

"It was built and owned by two brothers, Manuel and Duarte. I knew them both. In fact, I saw them building it. They used the local stone and began by putting up a large stable; then each of them built his own living quarters to right and left of it. It was all pretty rough, but it was solid—like themselves."

"Have you been out here long?" Lady Grantly asked.

"On and off, all my life. My mother was Portuguese and owned a house quite near here. I was often here as a boy. That's how I came to know Manuel and Duarte."

"Where are they now?"

"Duarte went to Mozambique about ten years ago and died there. His half share of the house passed to his brother Manuel, and it was Manuel who had the conversion done and sold the house to you. He's now farming in Angola. Shall we go and look at the house?"

Lady Grantly rose. "That would be lovely."

"I'll drive you out," Mr. Weybridge said, "but I'll tell your chauffeur to go to the house and wait for you. I'm afraid I shall be busy with a client, so I can't drive you back to Sintra."

"Couldn't your secretary go with us and save you the trouble?" Lady Grantly suggested.

"Milou doesn't like to leave the office while Senhor Melo is away. Shall we go?"

They went out into the sunny street and he paused to give an order to Alípio. Then he led them to his car—pale yellow and powerful, of the type designed to take two people of normal size in front and two pygmies behind.

"I think Lady Grantly had better sit in front with me; it's more comfortable," he explained.

He settled her in and then opened the door at the back for Emma, holding the two dogs back until she was in.

"Don't let them get onto the seat," he requested. "They know it's forbidden, but they'll have a try."

They had several tries. Finding Emma resolute, they

struggled for a place on her lap and compromised by sharing it.

"If they annoy you," Robert Weybridge said over his shoulder, turning the car towards the shopping district, "shout at them. They're called Brush and Bruno. You won't mind," he went on to Lady Grantly, "if I collect one or two things from the shops on our way?"

"Of course not. It's very kind of you to take us to the house," Lady Grantly said.

They stopped at the butcher's, and at a signal from the car's musical horn—the first five notes of "John Peel"—a boy came hurrying out with two large plastic bags and a plastic carrier. Some of the contents looked like dog meat, but Emma could also see a large sirloin of beef and a leg of lamb. The bags were placed at her feet, and she was requested by Mr. Weybridge to keep the dogs' noses out of them. They then went on to a grocer's, where a cardboard container full of groceries was placed on the seat beside Emma. Proceeding to the market, they took delivery of an enormous fish whose tail stuck out of the plastic bag into which it had been put.

"Wait a minute; we'll need some newspapers round that," Robert Weybridge said. "Otherwise the dogs will smell of fish for days."

Wrapped in newspapers, the fish was placed beside the meat on the floor of the car. Emma, who had detected a false note in the excuse of the client who was going to keep Mr. Weybridge busy, was now convinced that this had been a fiction designed to save him the trouble of driving back to Sintra.

"I think that's all. Now we can get on," he said.

"You've forgotten the vegetables," Emma said. "I could fit a cabbage on my lap between the dogs' heads."

He turned and subjected her to a steady stare. "Perhaps you'd like me to put Lady Grantly at the back and you in the front?" he suggested.

"No. You just come and sit with the dogs and the fish, and I'll drive. I've got my English license with me."

To this he made no reply, merely telling Lady Grantly that the drive would take just under half an hour.

The first part of the journey was downhill, leaving behind the hills of Sintra and crossing the valley beyond. Then there was a gentle rise and a run along a beautiful, pine-shaded road with occasional glimpses of a blue sea. Little villages flashed by; hens fled squawking, donkeys plodded slowly on. Unlike Alípio, Robert Weybridge had nothing to tell them of the places they passed. One village, he seemed to think, was very much like the last, and though the scenery was charming, there was no point in echoing Lady Grantly's delight in it.

After driving for about twenty minutes, they slowed and turned into a shady lane. A hundred yards along it was a granite wall and an arched entrance.

"This is where I live," Mr. Weybridge said. "Will you forgive me if I drop these things?"

"Of course not. What a lovely house!" Lady Grantly exclaimed.

They had driven under the archway into a cool, cobbled courtyard. Before them was a large house built of stone. At the John Peel signal, a manservant appeared and removed the shopping and, to Emma's relief, the dogs. Robert Weybridge did not get out, but before driving away, proffered what Emma thought a very lukewarm invitation to go in and have some coffee. She was relieved to hear Lady Grantly refuse.

"You're very kind, but I think we ought to get on, don't you?"

Mr. Weybridge, already getting on, said that they must come and dine with him as soon as they had settled into their house. No pretense of any eager anticipation, Emma noted, and wished there had been a blunt instrument at hand.

"We're getting near your village, Aldeia da Torre," he said. "Your house, Casa da Torre, is named after the tower you'll see as we go past—it's a ruin now, but it dates from the twelfth century. It's a pretty little village, and nice and quiet."

But when they reached it, it looked far from quiet. From end to end of its single street, young men and women were strolling, dressed in garments as colourful as they were scanty. Most of them were wearing locally purchased straw hats; a few were barefooted. Mr. Weybridge slowed the car to walking pace and threaded a way through them.

"Summer school," he explained. "Painters. They're leaving tomorrow."

"And do more come?" Lady Grantly asked.

"No."

"Are they in camp?"

"No. They're staying at the house of a Portuguese painter named Augusto Tavares. Have you heard of him?"

"No, I don't think I have. Does he have a summer school every year?"

"No. This was the first. It'll be the last. It wasn't a success. He's very poor, is Augusto, and every now and then he wakes up with a wonderful idea for making money. This was one of them. He spent a lot on advertising and got together the crowd you're looking at now. English, French and Spanish." He got the car clear and increased its speed. "But he made the mistake of fixing an all-in fee for board, lodging and tuition. Most of them bypassed the tuition and concentrated on the food and the wine."

"Does he live here all the time, or only in summer?"

"All the time. He's about my age. I was going to say we played together as boys, but he wasn't keen on games. He was a dreamy type. He liked to sit round under trees, like Ferdinand the Bull. My mother was sure he was a genius, and so was he—but somehow he never succeeded in making it pay off." He stopped and pointed. "Your house, Lady Grantly."

It was at the end of the narrow road into which they had turned. Beyond it was the sea. As they came nearer, Emma saw that although the photographs had shown a great deal, they had given no idea of the odd, charming shape of the building. And no photographs could have prepared them for the warmth and the scent and the beauty of the garden and the trees surrounding it.

The design of the house was simple—the stable had been made into two spacious rooms, drawing room and dining room, both with enormous windows looking over the sea. In the wing which the brother Manuel had occupied were now three bedrooms and two bathrooms; at the late Duarte's side were the kitchen and the maids' rooms. An outhouse, its roof tiles matching those of the main building, was the garage, and attached to it was a wash house with a large stone tank. All the floors were of gleaming parquet; every window was framed by wisteria or bougainvillia. In the garden were hibiscus and oleander, a grape-hung arbour, roses and geraniums and two pepper trees. At the end of the garden was a well—seldom used now that water was laid on, but kept, Mr. Weybridge told them, because it was picturesque.

Alípio had fetched the maids from the village, and they were waiting, dark-skinned, smiling, short and sturdy, both with glossy black hair drawn back into a plait that curled round the back of their heads. They followed Lady Grantly round the rooms, clearly proud of its cleanliness, which Robert Weybridge said was the result of the work they had been doing in it since they had been engaged.

Emma left them after a time and walked out onto the terrace that ran the length of the house in front. She was feeling dazed—perhaps drunk, she thought. For the much-travelled Lady Grantly, this semi-tropical luxuriance was probably nothing new; for herself, the limit of whose journeying had been a walking tour in the Trossachs, the scene was a revelation. She had never seen nature so brilliantly, so extravagantly painted; she had never seen light so clear.

She drew a deep breath, taking in not only happiness but also reassurance; she could leave Lady Grantly here and go away without misgivings. This was a home and a haven.

She became aware that Robert Weybridge was standing beside her.

"Like it?" he enquired.

"Who wouldn't?"

"I'm just off. If there's anything you want at any time, just—"

"—ask Milou. It was nice of you to bring us along with the shopping."

There was a pause.

"Will you be staying out here long?" he asked.

"No. I've just come to see Lady Grantly settled."

"And you think she'll be happy here?"

"I'm absolutely certain she will."

"And not lonely?"

"She'll soon get to know people. Before I leave, I'll take her along to see Mr. and Mrs. Cooper."

He looked at her with surprise. "You know them?"

"I've met their son. They're living just across there, aren't they?"

"Yes. Would you say they were likely to become friends of Lady Grantly?"

"Never having met them, I wouldn't say anything. But their son told me that Mr. Cooper isn't very well, and he thought—"

"I've seen them several times in the office. He looked to me the picture of health. His wife, on the other hand . . . You're sure you didn't get it wrong?"

"Quite sure."

"And you think that they might become friends as well as neighbours?"

"Why shouldn't they?"

"Different background, different outlook, different way of life altogether. They've sent away all the servants. They've even sold the car their son bought them. They asked Senhor Melo to write out for them the exact pronunciation of the numbers one to ten, so that they could phone for a taxi when they needed one. They sacked the gardener, and Mr. Cooper's doing his best to grow catmint and hollyhocks."

"Why shouldn't he, if he wants to? It's his garden, isn't it?"

"Of course. I'm merely pointing out certain basic differences which might operate against this friendly-neighbours policy of yours." He studied her meditatively. "Did anybody ever tell you that you're the aggressive type?"

"Never. You're the first. Has anyone ever wrapped you up in newspaper with some fish and parked you between two

Great Danes? I can't see why you bothered to bring us out here."

"In the absence of Senhor Melo, it was my duty. And—"

"And Milou doesn't like to leave the office while he's away. I forgot."

"My work is confined to the legal side. Anything domestic is—"

"—taken care of by Milou. I must remember to tell Lady Grantly."

"Do that. This has been a charming acquaintance. I'm sorry it's to end so soon. But perhaps before it ends, you'd tell me why you're so worried about Lady Grantly. She seems to me perfectly well able to manage her affairs adequately." He glanced at her left hand. "Are you going back to get married?"

"Yes."

"In that case—"

He stopped. Lady Grantly had come on to the terrace to join them.

"Thank you again, Mr. Weybridge," she said. "It's all quite perfect. Just the right size, such a nice shape, with this lovely terrace in front to enjoy the sun, and that little veranda at the back when the sun gets too hot. It couldn't be nicer. And Emma tells me that there are people called Cooper living next door—isn't that nice, to have English neighbours? She's called Nancy."

"Nancy's the daughter," Mr. Weybridge said.

"Oh, there's a daughter too, is there?"

"And a son," Emma told her. "But they're not here."

"But you said they were."

"The father and mother are here."

"Mother, father, Mr. and Mrs. Cooper, daughter and son. Six of them. Quite a family. I shall enjoy meeting them."

Emma, glancing at Mr. Weybridge, noted the look of mystification on his face. That would teach him, she thought with satisfaction. Now he'd realize she hadn't come out here just for the ride.

"We're keeping Mr. Weybridge," Lady Grantly said. "Goodbye, then, and thank you once again for finding me such a lovely house."

"I'm afraid I can't claim any credit for that," he said. "It was a man named Delmont who—"

"Oh, do you know him?"

"I've had a good deal of correspondence with him."

"Which one?" Lady Grantly enquired. "There are two, you know—father and son. I don't care for either of them, but I don't think they're likely to come out here."

Mr. Weybridge seemed about to say something, decided against it, and took his leave. There was nothing for Lady Grantly and Emma to do but lock the house and then return to Lisbon.

They spent the interval before the arrival of the furniture in sight-seeing. Alípio was useful and informative, but he seemed to invent frequent and very thin excuses to go out to Aldeia da Torre. When Emma wondered why, Lady Grantly enlightened her.

"The maid, Emma. The younger one—what was her name?"

"Lourdes."

"She was eyeing him. He's a good-looking young fellow. I can see it's going to be just like Barbados. My mother was always taking young couples off to be married. She said it was the climate. Do you know, Emma, this place suits you beautifully; you're looking remarkably well."

"Would you like me to ring up Mrs. Cooper and fix a date for a meeting?"

"Not until we're living in the house. Let's enjoy everything we can in Lisbon. There isn't much time before the furniture comes."

It arrived a week later. There was some delay before it was cleared by the Customs, but the day of the move was finally fixed for the third of June. When the day came, Lady Grantly and Emma packed all they could into the car and left the rest to be collected by Alípio on a second trip. They drove out to the house, and the furniture trucks, carrying three enormous containers, arrived an hour later, turning with difficulty into the narrow road and lining up as near the house as possible. Then the unloading began.

A halt was called for lunch. Alípio was instructed to take the men to the village and see that they were fed. The maids made themselves a cauldron of soup. Emma went on to the terrace to unpack the picnic lunch she had ordered for herself and Lady Grantly from the hotel. She was taking some rolls out of their wrapping, when a nervous cough sounded behind her. Turning, she saw a short, round little man with Nancy Cooper's round brown eyes and button nose.

"Mr. Cooper," she said unhesitatingly, and understood Robert Weybridge's surprise at being told he was unfit; nobody had ever looked more robust. He was holding a tray covered with a white cloth. Putting it on the newly arrived glass-topped garden table, he backed away and mumbled a shy explanation.

"Bit o' something to eat. The missis saw your furniture and we knew you'd 'ave nowhere to cook, just yet."

"That's very, very kind," Emma said warmly, and went to

call Lady Grantly. "Look"—she indicated the tray—"food sent over by Mrs. Cooper."

"How do you do?" Lady Grantly shook his hand vigorously. "I never in my life heard anything so kind."

"Good cook, she is," he said, wiping the moisture of embarrassment from his brow. " 'Ope you enjoy it. 'Bye for now."

When he had vanished among the pine trees, they lifted the cloth.

"Stew with dumplings. Oh dear!" said Lady Grantly. "What's under the other—"

"Cornflour blancmange."

There was a pause.

"So kind of her," Lady Grantly said firmly at last. "And cooked by herself. If it weren't such a very warm day . . . How many dumplings do you think you could manage?"

Emma was about to say that she couldn't manage any, when she saw that two gaunt and ribby dogs, their noses lifted to take in the appetizing odour, had crept round the corner of the house and were waiting with mingled hope and fear. The feast was shared with them. The stew was delicious, the dumplings feather-light, the blancmange creamy; the thought of Mrs. Cooper spending the morning in a hot kitchen, preparing it all, made Emma even more disinclined to eat it.

The dogs, for once filled, went away.

"And now, back to work," Lady Grantly said.

By nightfall, the furniture containers were empty. Two were removed by the men; the third was left beside the outhouse, to be disposed of by Alípio to a man in the village who had expressed a wish to buy it. The next day was spent in arranging the furniture, and gradually the rooms took on a lived-in air. Carpets went down, pictures went up, two women from the village carried off curtains to be altered to the new measurements. And as soon as the maids showed signs of being able to work without supervision, Lady Grantly proceeded to inspect the village and its surroundings, going on tours of exploration which she called getting the scent. She harangued, in clear and loud English, the owners of too-thin cats, and exhorted them to feed them. She bought an enormous bird cage and then bought all the birds which she saw being kept in tiny, cramped cages on the walls of the village houses. She instructed the village butcher to give bones to all the gaunt dogs and to send her the bill. And Emma, sometimes accompanying her, sometimes staying at home, counted the days and tried to forget that each one brought her nearer to departure.

"Do you feel like walking across to the Coopers' house?" she asked Lady Grantly one morning.

"That's a good idea. But not unannounced, Emma. Will you telephone and suggest eleven o'clock?"

Mr. Cooper, answering, said that eleven o'clock would be a very good time to come. As an afterthought, he said that he would inform his wife.

They walked through the cool pine wood and found Mr. Cooper, hot and perspiring, at work in the garden. He welcomed them with shy pleasure and went inside to fetch his wife.

She was as shy as her husband, very thin and small and pale. She moved and spoke with a kind of grim determination, and her greeting to Lady Grantly had an appealing directness.

"Nice of you to come," she said. "We 'aven't spoken to a soul except ourselves for the past week. Come in 'ere; it's cooler."

The room into which she ushered them had been made, Emma guessed, as nearly a replica of their Silver Street living room as possible. It adjoined the kitchen and had a round table in the middle, covered with a plush cloth. The carpet was red, with pale pink roses embossed in each corner. The windows looked onto a cement yard. They were trying, Mrs. Cooper explained, to get things more homelike; they had not liked to change anything until their son Len had gone back to England, but once on their own, had set about altering the rooms to suit themselves. And what Mrs. Cooper had done in the house, her husband was attempting to do in the garden, but with less hope of success, for it was doubtful whether he would ever subdue it to the level of his little front lawn of Silver Street days. But like his wife, he was busy all the day long, and almost happy. He had a plan for new flower beds and borrowed a pencil from Emma to show her where he was going to put them.

Conversation did not flag. Lady Grantly, finding both husband and wife natural and unpretentious, was at her best, communicative and friendly and full of plans in which they seemed to be included. Walking home with Emma at the end of the visit, she expressed her liking for them both.

"Simple, and *good*," she said. "And lonely, poor things. I shall drop in frequently, and you must do the same, and we must get them into the way of dropping in to see us."

Emma said nothing. She had six days left. It seemed incredible that she would soon wake up one morning and find herself staring out at chimneys across a narrow London street. No more flowers, unless Gerald presented her with some, or she went to look at them in the parks. No more colour flaunting itself round her as she ate breakfast under a pepper tree. And back to house-hunting, for Gerald had written to tell her that the house they had decided to buy had been filched from under his nose. They were back at the starting gate.

His letters had come every day—short, pithy, to the point—dictated to his secretary, with a personal note added at the end in his own handwriting. Her replies had not been easy to write; he had no interest in the things she was doing here and was concerned only in what they were to do on her return.

"I haven't long left," she reminded Lady Grantly as they neared the house.

"Emma, don't talk about going."

"But I must. I'm glad I came out, because I'll be able to picture you out here and—"

"When the time comes for you to go, I suppose I shall have to face it. But don't let's *anticipate*."

They had reached the house. A maid who had seen them approaching was waiting to tell them that a Portuguese gentleman had called; she had shown him into the drawing room.

"Come with me, Emma," Lady Grantly requested. "If he doesn't speak English or French, I shall be lost."

But the visitor spoke grammatically correct English, though with a pronunciation so strange that it was difficult to understand him. He was a man in his late thirties, tall, with long hair, a long, mournful face and a long, drooping moustache. On a table he had placed a wide-brimmed straw hat; below it was a portfolio. As they entered, he gave a ceremonious bow and addressed Lady Grantly.

"Madam, good morning. Please forgive me for making this visit. I wished to speak with you on an important matter. My name is Augusto Tavares."

"Oh, how nice. Do sit down," Lady Grantly invited. "This is Miss Challis, who is staying with me."

"I will not sit, madam, because I am in my professional capacity. I have brought with me some paintings for you to look at. Some are my own work, others"—he was drawing them out of the portfolio—"are the work of my pupils. And it is their work which I should like you to examine. Look!"

They looked. There were oils and water colours, landscapes, seascapes, portraits, still lifes and nudes. One he left to the last and then held it up triumphantly.

"And tell me, madam, what is this?"

"Oh!" Lady Grantly gave an exclamation of delight. "Look, Emma, it's this house. Did you do this, Senhor Tavares?"

"I did it, and for you, madam. When my friend Robert told me that there was a charming English lady coming to this house, I thought that I would prepare a present of welcome. It is from myself to yourself. Will you accept it?"

"I should love it! You shouldn't have dreamt of doing it, but it was a charming thought. Do sit down, won't you?"

"I am still in my professional capacity, madam. I came not only to make my little presentation. I came also with a proposal. It is that I shall teach you to paint. I ask that you will make yourself my pupil."

"But . . ." Lady Grantly sought a chair for herself. "I haven't touched a paintbrush since I married. I gave it up at my husband's request; he thought it was a great waste of canvas. I don't think I could even hold a brush after all these years!"

"You must begin again, madam."

"At my age!"

He looked genuinely horrified. "Age? Age, madam? Can

you speak of age in the same breath with Art? Did Casals say, 'I am old, I will not play?' Did Michelangelo say, 'I am seventy years old, I will not finish my design for the Julian Tomb?' When Renoir could not hold his brushes, did he cease to paint? Did Chaplin, Carlos, Charlie say, 'I am old, I will produce no more films, no more babies?' No!"

This negative was accompanied by a thump on the table. Then he paused, looking spent.

"You don't understand, Senhor Tavares," Lady Grantly began. "I—"

"Madam, I am offering to conduct you back to the Art which your husband interrupted. My summer school has terminated, and I am going to amass private pupils, because I have thought like this: When foreigners, cultured people like yourself, come to live here, what are they going to do? They are not young. They will not play tennis, or walk many miles with their dogs. They must occupy themselves with something; they cannot sit forever on a terrace to look at the sea. So what better, what more engaging than to set up an easel and begin to create? But not without a guide. They will become discouraged. They will grieve. They will put away the easel. Then there is nothing left but to sit on the terrace to look at the sea."

He paused to recover.

"But, Senhor Tavares," Lady Grantly pointed out, "isn't that just what we've all come out here to do? What is more pleasant, more suitable for the elderly than to sit on the terrace and look at the sea?"

"It is death," pronounced Senhor Tavares. "It is slow death. I would not like it for my worst enemy. Some will tell you that I am seeking pupils because I am poor and need to have money. This is true, but I do not want you to be my pupil only for that. I wish to help you. Once you have consented, I will go to Lisbon with you and you shall buy easel, brushes, everything. Will you be my pupil, madam?"

"Well, I . . . Do sit down, Senhor Tavares. You look so hot."

"I am not yet engaged, madam. In my professional capacity, I do not care—"

"Well, it seems rather absurd, but perhaps we could arrange a lesson or two, and then you could see how hopeless I am."

"The more bad, the more to teach. I will take this talent that your husband saw so despisingly, and I will make it grow up. Here is my paper with the charge, madam. It is, of course, in advance, but you will soon congratulate yourself on the decision you have made. I shall come here at eleven o'clock on every Wednesday and Friday morning. We will work in this room, or in the garden when it is cool. If any of your friends wish to join, we shall make a little group. It is a pity that this young lady is going away. Robert told me that she is here for a short time only. I would have liked to paint so interesting a face. I should have called it 'Serenity.' "

This surprised Emma, whose feelings, by this time, she would have expected to be written clearly on her face. They were not serene. Here was the first of the sharks, this self-styled master with a Basset-hound expression and a bull-terrier persistence. Here was the first bear coming to lick the honeypot. And Lady Grantly would hold out, as she had held out just now, to the point where poverty was mentioned, and then she would capitulate. The word would get round. Somebody would be along soon to give her piano lessons.

But Senhor Tavares, departing with his portfolio, left behind him more than a picture of the house; Lady Grantly began to enthuse over the coming lessons. She had forgotten

Renoir and Michelangelo, but had remembered Grandma Moses; she would have driven straight off to Lisbon to choose a comfortable camp stool if she had not sent Alípio and the car to take the transportless Senhor Tavares back to his home.

"I must write down the days of those lessons, Emma. Lend me a pencil, will you?"

Failing to find her pencil, Emma produced a pen from the writing desk. Watching Lady Grantly making notes, she tried to remember when she had last had the pencil. It was a gold one, a present from Gerald; she seldom used it and would not miss it, but it would be awkward if it were lost. Searching her memory, she thought that the last time she had had it was at the Coopers'; then she remembered that Mr. Cooper had borrowed it to make a rough sketch of the future flower beds. Had he given it back?

She assumed that he had, but she had not found it when she went to bed that night; nor did it come to light during the next few days. But while she was watching Senhor Tavares and Lady Grantly settling down to their first lesson, a maid came to tell her that she was wanted on the telephone. She picked up the receiver and heard Mrs. Cooper's voice. It sounded oddly strained.

"Miss Challis?"

"Yes."

"I just wanted . . . 'ave you lost anything?"

"Have I what?"

"Lost anything. Missed anything?"

"No, I don't . . . Oh, yes. My little gold pencil. But—"

"Can you come over 'ere? Now, if it's convenient. 'E's gorn out to the village."

Mystified and rather uneasy, she put down the receiver

and went straight over to the house. Mrs. Cooper was wait-ing for her.

"Come in," she said, and led the way inside. As soon as they were in the living room, she held out a small package. " 'Ere it is," she said.

"Thank you. But—"

"Sit down, Miss Challis, please. I've got to explain."

Emma, on whom light had begun to dawn, spoke gently. "You don't have to, you know, Mrs. Cooper."

"I don't 'ave to, no. But I'm going to. It'll get it off my chest. If you miss anything ever again, like your pencil, just come straight over 'ere and tell me. 'E just takes things, that's all; 'e doesn't know when I give them back."

She paused, staring at the paper fan which decorated the empty fireplace. Then she began her explanation in a dull monotone.

" 'E used to do it a bit when 'e was a youngster, four or five. They'd find things under 'is pillow. They treated it as a joke, like, because they didn't know about mind specialists and that. You didn't go running to 'em then like you do now-adays. So 'is family just laughed and said 'e'd grow up a fine pickpocket and be able to support them all. And whether it was because they didn't make no fuss, just took it natural, I don't know—but 'e grew out of it. After 'e was six, 'e never 'ad 'is 'ands on a thing, and nobody reminded 'im about it because they'd always said it would stop. I know all this because when it came on, just after we got to that 'ouse in Amersham, I went and 'ad a talk with 'is brother Arthur, and Arthur told me. I thought I'd better 'ave a doctor. The doctor said it was shock, kind of. Everything 'ad 'appened too sud-den. Len thought maybe it was too much excitement, all those people after Nancy. But myself, I think it was the money that did it. You can't understand, Miss Challis, because you're not our sort, what it meant to 'im, a decent working man who'd always worked 'ard to keep 'is family until they was old enough to earn for themselves—you don't know what it was like for 'im to see all that money being lashed about, a car 'ere, a 'ouse, clothes we didn't need, presents we didn't want. It was nice to see the kids so excited and 'appy, but all that spending went to 'is stomach. Easy come, easy go, Len kept telling 'im, but you couldn't get Dad to see it that way. To 'im, it was all wicked waste. If 'e'd kept on with 'is work, 'e might 'ave been all right, but the kids made 'im retire, and 'e 'ad nothing to do but 'ang about, and I think 'e brooded. That's when it came on. The doctor said not to tell 'im anything, just to give the things back, and get 'im right away from all the things that was worrying 'im. Get out of the country, 'e said, get where you won't see your daughter on the telly, where you won't see any of the moneyspending crowd, where you'll be on your own. So we told Dad we was coming for my sake, because I was run down. And so we're 'ere, and I've tried to make things the way he's used to 'aving them, and that's all I can do. I'm sorry about your pencil."

There was a long silence.

"Do you think that being out here has done him any good?"

"It's too early to say. But Lady Grantly being so friendly, that's 'elped. It's 'elped him and it's 'elped me too."

Emma, walking thoughtfully back through the pine wood, wondered how much she should tell Lady Grantly, and decided to leave the matter until the last moment before her departure. She remembered with gratitude Mrs. Cooper's parting words. They had not spoken of Lady Grantly until Emma had said goodbye. Then:

"When are you off?" Mrs. Cooper had enquired.

"The day after tomorrow."

"I know you're worried about 'er, but you needn't be. I'll keep an eye on 'er. She'll be all right."

Yes, she would, Emma thought. Friends, and hobbies. There was nothing to stay for.

She saw Alípio washing the car and stopped to enquire somewhat impatiently when he was going to arrange for the removal of the furniture crate, still standing where it had been put beside the outhouse. He would see about it tomorrow, he told her; there had been a delay because the man had not agreed to a fair price.

The evening was one of the warmest there had been since their arrival in Portugal; at Emma's suggestion, they had dinner outside. It was so still that the only sound seemed to be the rise and fall of the waves against the cliffs. The lighted house looked like a stage set. Emma felt wrapped in peace—but suddenly Lady Grantly spoke out of the semi-darkness, and the note in her voice went to Emma's heart.

"Why do you have to go away? You can't be serious about marrying that man. I can't believe it, I can't, I can't. You're going to be very unhappy, and that's going to make me unhappy. Look how well everything is going out here. Just look at this lovely little house, and—"

"That's what's making it easier to leave you. I promise to come out and stay with you whenever I can."

"He won't let you."

"Of course he will. Don't you want to see me married and settled?"

"Not married to that man. People think I'm a silly old woman, but I've had a lot of experience and I can see you're making a dreadful mistake. You're too good for him. If he knew it, I'd think there was some hope for him—but he doesn't know it. I know it, and I think you're throwing yourself away."

"If I promise to come out regularly and see you—"

"It'll never, never be the same. Never. I'm not being selfish; don't think that. I'm not thinking of myself—at least, I'm trying not to. I'm only thinking of you and your happiness."

It was a long time before Emma could calm her. When at last she succeeded, they walked slowly round the garden, saying nothing.

And it was while they were passing the veranda on their way into the house that Lady Grantly called Emma's attention to the tin trunks.

Chapter
6

There were three of them standing in a corner of the veranda at the back of the house. They were small and had curved tops. Two of them were bright yellow, the third a peculiarly bilious shade of green. All were scratched and battered, bound with ropes, their locks hanging broken and useless. Emma went in to ask the maids what they were doing out there and came back to Lady Grantly to report.

"Not theirs," she said. "They know nothing about them."

"Then they must be Alípio's."

"Why should he bring luggage? He doesn't live here."

"Did you ask him?"

"How could I? He wasn't there. The maids said you'd given him permission to go home early."

"So I did. He said he wanted to visit some relations."

"Shall I have the trunks taken into the outhouse?"

"I don't think that would be wise; they might be forgotten. Leave them here, and someone will come and claim them. Why they should be lying there if they don't belong to any of us, I can't imagine. I daresay we shall find out in the morning."

While Emma was undressing, she thought she heard sounds outside the house. She put on a dressing gown and went out onto the veranda. No light showed from the kitchen; the maids had gone to their rooms. She switched on a garden light which enabled her to see as far as the gate, but there was nobody in sight. Then, turning to go back to her room, she saw to her amazement that one of the trunks had been opened; its lid was now half closed, and the sleeves of a garment were hanging out.

She was puzzled and angry, and beneath these emotions was uneasiness as she remembered how the maids had answered her questions about the trunks. Their denials had been too loud, too hasty—or was she imagining it? Whether they had known anything or not, nothing more could be done tonight.

When she glanced out early the following morning, the trunks had vanished. Relieved, she went into the garden and had coffee and toast at a table under a shady tree. It was only half-past eight, but the heat was already becoming uncomfortable, and for the first time, she missed a beach near by to which she could go for a swim.

The maids seemed to be making a great deal of noise, but it was nice noise, she thought lazily; when would she be able to sit in the shade again listening to maids going about their work? When would she next feel heat pricking her skin? It was all but over. She had to go away, but she would go with a feeling of thankfulness for having been granted these weeks of carefree leisure.

She might have sat on, dreaming, if she had not been roused by an odour that was at first faint and then so strong as to drive her to go towards the kitchen to investigate. Why would they be filling the garden with the smell of garlic at this time of the morning?

She turned the corner of the house—and then came to an abrupt stop and stood wondering if she could be dreaming.

The large wooden furniture container which Alípio had been so long in removing was still pushed against the out-house, its open end facing the house. It made a spacious shelter. Inside it, seated on the wooden floor and eating from a communal dish, were a woman and five children. The eldest was eight or nine, the youngest about three. The woman was young and could have been beautiful, but she looked thin and exhausted, with large, tragic black eyes and hair that straggled from a loosely tied knot. She looked across the steaming dish and caught sight of Emma, and paused for a few moments with a tin spoon halfway to her mouth. Then lowering her eyes and hunching her shoulders in an effort to make herself smaller, she went on with her meal, feeding herself and the youngest child alternately. The others, seemingly starved, bent over the dish, lost to everything but assuaging their hunger.

She went into the kitchen. Who, she asked the maids, was the woman, and what was she doing here? She was aware, as she asked the questions, that both maids had been expecting her queries and that she was not going to be given any information. They shrugged their shoulders and raised help-less hands; they knew nothing. When had the woman come? They did not know; when they looked out of the kitchen window this morning, she was already there, in the luggage container, preparing food. Who was she? They did not know. Did she belong to the village? No. They had never seen her before.

Emma went back to her room, allowed a reasonable interval to elapse and then went to see the woman. The meal was over. One of the children had drawn water from the well and was washing the tin plates. The woman was pushing the small clay stove on which the food had been cooked into a corner. There were more pitiful details to be observed—the rough cotton sheets which had been spread on some straw to make beds, the watery, high-smelling soup that remained at the bottom of the dish, and in the depths of the crate, the tin trunks which had been reposing on the veranda.

The woman began folding the sheets, her glance sliding away from Emma's.

"Who are you?" Emma asked her in Spanish.

There was no reply. The woman merely gazed at her with a panic-stricken expression and then slowly shook her head. Tears began to pour down her cheeks. The youngest child, seeing them, set up a howl. The other four came to stand behind the woman. She must be the mother, Emma decided, but there was no visible likeness to her in any of them. Still weeping, she picked up the crying child and rocked it in her arms; it became quiet, and she put it down and went on folding the sheets. It was clear that nothing more would be forthcoming in the way of information.

Lady Grantly was calling from the terrace. Emma found her sitting on a wicker chair, admiring the view.

"Good morning, Emma. Did you have a good breakfast?"

"Never mind breakfast. We have a problem," Emma told her. "The tin trunks have been claimed. They belong to a woman with five children, and she has just given them breakfast, but not a good one—a wishy-washy sort of soup smelling of garlic with bread floating about in it."

"Oh, was that the strong smell?"

"Yes."

"Are they in the kitchen?"

"No. They're squatters."

"*Squatters?*"

"That's the only word I can think of."

"But where are they squatting?"

"In the large furniture container the men didn't take away—the one Alípio said he was going to sell to a man in the village."

"Alípio? Do you mean to say that Alípio has installed a woman and five children in my empty crate? I must go and look."

They walked round to the veranda. The children were seated round the woman, watching her sorting the contents of one of the trunks. She was still crying, making no sound, the tears dropping onto her hands or onto the clothes she was folding.

"Who is she?" Lady Grantly asked, after a long and fascinated survey.

"Nobody knows. The maids disclaim all knowledge. I tried her in Spanish and made her cry. We'll have to wait until Alípio comes and see if he knows anything about them, but somehow I don't feel he's responsible for this."

"He may be, Emma, he may be. I don't suppose for a moment that a handsome young man like that has lived like a *monk*. He might quite well have fathered a family."

"He could hardly have a child nine years old."

"Well, perhaps not. Just look at the neat way everything is arranged in there. But those children look terribly thin. Don't you think I'd better—"

"No. You're not going to do anything. Not yet, anyway,"

Emma said firmly. "Come and sit in the garden until Alípio comes."

But when he came, his horror at the sight of the little household in the crate was only equalled by his astonishment at being asked for information. He spread his hands as widely as the maids had spread theirs, but Emma felt that this time the disclaimer might be genuine.

"You asked the maids, miss?"

"Yes. They know nothing—so they say."

"I will ask. They will tell me."

He went round to the veranda. Emma followed him, and Lady Grantly was not far behind. Alípio bypassed the crate and called the two maids, who came out and stood looking apprehensive.

What followed was brief. The woman came out of the crate to listen to what was being said and from time to time broke into wild cries of denial or lamentation. Then, coming closer, she began to address Alípio in a tear-choked voice. The children gathered round and one by one began to howl. The voices of the maids rose, Alípio yelled, the woman wailed.

"*Stop* it!" Emma shouted suddenly, and brought a sudden silence, broken only by the children's sobs. "Now. Alípio, who is she and what is she doing here?"

"She is an imposter," Alípio said sullenly. "Send her away. I will go for the police myself and—"

"I asked you who she is."

"She does not say. You must not let her stay here, miss, or she will make trouble. Let me go and bring the police. That will frighten her."

"Won't she tell you who she is?"

"No, miss."

He was obviously lying. Emma was about to tell him so,

when Lady Grantly spoke in a loud and authoritative voice.

"Nobody is going to bring any police here," she announced. "Not until those children have got some flesh on their poor little bones. Emma, this is a matter for a lawyer. Please telephone to Mr. Weybridge and ask him if he will come here and explain what it's all about."

Emma telephoned and was told by a polite manservant that Mr. Weybridge was out.

"In that case," said Lady Grantly, "you must drive to Sintra, to the office of that other lawyer—what was his name?"

"Senhor Melo. He's away."

"He was. He might be back. It's a pity he chose such an awkward time to go away. But if he isn't there, Mr. Weybridge is sure to be. Tell him that I'd be grateful if he'd come here, but you must make it clear that there's to be no talk of police or anything of that kind. Go now, Emma; we must get to the bottom of this."

Alípio brought round the car.

"Why don't you come with me?" Emma asked Lady Grantly.

"No. I am going to stay here to see that nobody shouts at that poor creature again. If we both go, how do we know that the maids won't put this woman and those poor starved children outside the gate? Hurry, Emma. I'm sorry to send you out in this dreadful heat."

It was almost unbearable. There was not a breath of wind. The comparative coolness of early morning had gone, leaving a burning feeling in the air. As Emma was getting into the car, she saw the maids closing the shutters of all the doors and windows, and the wisdom of this became apparent when she was borne along at Alípio's usual high speed and felt the hot wind blowing in onto her cheeks.

"Try Mr. Weybridge's house as you go past," she ordered. "He may have come home."

The shade of the courtyard, as they drove in, afforded her temporary relief. But Mr. Weybridge was not in. She told Alípio to drive to Sintra.

It was cooler in Sintra, and cooler still in Senhor Melo's office. Milou, in a sleeveless linen dress, unruffled and efficient, said she would help if she could, but Senhor Melo was still away and she could not leave the office. Mr. Weybridge would be the person to go to.

"I went. He was not at home. Are you sure he isn't away, too?"

"He spoke with me in this office yesterday," Milou assured her. "Perhaps he went out only for a little while. If you return to his house, maybe he will be there."

It was unsatisfactory, but there was nothing to do but drive back. Once Sintra had been left behind, the heat came through the open windows of the car with the force of a blast furnace. Perspiration began to trickle down Emma's back; her face felt on fire. Mr. Weybridge's house had never looked so pleasant, so quiet, so well-tended; its trees shed a blessed shadow across the gardens to the right and left of the courtyard.

The same polite manservant, the same sickeningly familiar reply: Mr. Weybridge was out.

Emma turned and walked down the steps. She thought she heard a familiar sound coming from beyond this arched gateway. The car was standing in the shade and Alípio was standing beside it, holding open a door. She was about to get in when she paused. She stood quite still, and the sound she had heard was repeated—and this time she knew that there could be no mistake. On any other kind of day, she might have heard it without interest but today she was only too ready to recognize the sound of a splash.

It was worth investigating. She took a path which led in the direction of the sound. The servant who had opened the door had retreated when she had reached the bottom of the steps, but he might still be lurking; she began to hurry.

The path ended in a rose-covered archway and a low, wrought-iron gate. She pushed it open, took a few steps and then halted.

She was looking at a charming picture. Even as her rage began to rise, dimming her vision, she could acknowledge the beauty of the setting. A long swimming pool, its water clear and green, its banks terraced. Shady trees on one side; on the other, a paved terrace half-shaded by vines, furnished with long, gaily-covered chairs and small marble-topped tables. And settling down to recline in the longest and lowest chair, Mr. Weybridge, in a pair of bathing trunks, still dripping from his swim, his two dogs welcoming him and then dropping down panting by his side.

Drawing a deep, difficult breath, Emma took in more details. Every comfort: beer on ice, black and green olives in case he felt exhausted after his exercise. Cigarettes to calm his nerves, in case going in to the office yesterday had upset him. Towels of gigantic size and geometric design. Books, too, on a table by his side. A bell-rope hanging from a tree, within his reach. That would be to summon the dancing girls. All this, while she had come and been turned away and sent sweating to Sintra. All this, while people who needed his well-paid services whistled in vain.

The dogs alerted him. He turned, and she was to remember as long as she lived the scene: the man and the dogs, the clear green trembling pool, the deep shadows and the brilliant colours, and she was to try to forget what she must have looked like, her face flushed with heat and anger, perspiration making her dress cling to her, struggling for self-control and calmness enough to tell him what she thought of him.

"Why you . . . you . . . you *liar!*" she brought out at last. "You low-down, beastly, contemptible liar. You—"

He had risen. "Hey, steady on," he warned mildly.

"Sitting here like a . . . like a sultan, sitting and swimming on a nice shady terrace, pulling bells for somebody to come and dry you, swilling beer and lounging in comfort while your clients came to the door and got turned away. Lying here and getting an all-over tan while we chased round trying to get help. Splashing in a pool while we drove along baking, dusty streets. Taking fat fees from old ladies and leaving them to try and extricate themselves from howling women and five starving children while you lie here and—and—"

"Swill beer? Sit and swim?" he prompted in a calm tone.

"If you're trying to make excuses, don't. If Senhor Melo were here, do you think I'd waste one more minute looking at you taking your ease? But there's nobody else, and there she is and she won't say why, and the chauffeur won't say why, either, and I can only talk Spanish, which is no use, and if you knew how I felt, seeing you here in this—this glade, while that unfortunate woman and her children are huddled like rabbits in that crate, then you'd get some idea of what I think of you."

"I'm getting some idea. Do go on."

She went on because she knew that if she stopped, she would begin to cry, and she considered tears useless and no solution for any problem. But her voice was less steady.

"The trunks were there, the tin trunks, but we didn't know whose they were, and then this morning the woman was in the crate with all the children, feeding them on garlic soup. The maids know something, I'm certain they do. So does the chauffeur, but none of them will talk. So Lady Grantly wanted you to go and help, and I rang up but you were out, so I came here and you were still out, and I went to the office and came back here and then I heard a splash, and if I hadn't heard it, I'd never have known you were hiding in this place while your clients chased their tails. And if it's not too much to ask, perhaps you'd get dry and come out to—to—"

She stopped. She had forgotten the name of the house. She had forgotten the name of the village.

"To Lady Grantly's house, whatever it's called. You ought to know; you bought it for her. If she hadn't asked me to fetch you, I'd try and deal with this myself and leave you here and as far as I was concerned you could drown yourself in that pool."

"Thank you. Are you leaving?"

"Are you going to do anything to help?"

"To get a woman out of a crate?"

The colour left her cheeks. His tone was not angry, not even contemptuous; it was merely indifferent—and it was matched by his manner. He was wheeling his chair into the sun, spreading a towel, bringing some books and putting them at hand. For all the attention he was giving her, she might not have been there. A wave of humiliation swept over her, but it had a steadying effect. She spoke quietly.

"I'm sorry for trespassing, and for shouting at you," she said, "but I would have thought it was your job to help your clients out of difficulties."

He spoke as he rubbed suntan oil on his arms and shoulders. "When I came to an arrangement with Senhor Melo to deal with his English clients," he said, "I made the mistake of thinking that I would be acting as a lawyer. I was, of course, prepared to tie up a few strings—legal strings—if they arose later. What I wasn't prepared for was to be used as a wet nurse. The fees I charged were for my services in buying or selling houses. Anything else that was needed—servants, cars, chauffeur, electricity switched on or off, groceries ordered, language difficulties straightened out—that, I imagined, would be Senhor Melo's department. But the English clients, I discovered, didn't want to deal with Senhor Melo. They preferred to come to me. They showed a touching trust in my willingness to help them out of any small difficulty that came up at any time of the day. Or night. A lady came here one evening, when I was giving a dinner party, to complain that the village dogs were barking and disturbing her—would I do something? An elderly couple brought their cook and a list of their favourite foods, and begged me to translate the recipes. I was asked to recommend seamstresses and dressmakers. Anything that went wrong with the equipment in the houses was referred to me, with perhaps not so much violence as you used, but with force; it was, they said, my fault. People, after settling down, felt lonely; they came along to have what they called a chat. An Englishman who ought to have known better arrived with his swimming things and made himself at home on this terrace. I was out—really out—but that made no difference to his plan of passing a pleasant morning. Three girls who rented a house about two miles away called every morning to ask me to drive them to the market in Sintra. A dozen or more people came in from time to time to ask me when I was going to take them sight-seeing." He paused. "Would you like to say something at this point about my making excuses?"

"No."

"Then I shall go on. I took defensive action. I gave orders that I was to be at home to nobody. If Senhor Melo or Milou wanted me, they telephoned and I went to the office. My house became my own—for myself and for my friends. I do all the legal work for which I'm paid; I do it efficiently and conscientiously, but that is all I will do. The people who come out here are not children. They're, for the most part, travelled, experienced and perfectly able to cope with all the matters they preferred to refer to me. I've never before been asked to get a woman and five children out of a crate, but it doesn't really sound like a job for a lawyer. Will you mind if I don't see you to your car?"

Without answering, she turned and began to walk away. Then she stopped. When she turned back, he was still standing watching her.

"Suppose it *is* a job for a lawyer?" she suggested in a tone that she strove to keep calm. "How can you judge without knowing the facts?"

There was silence. He studied her without any change in his far-from-friendly expression. Then he nodded towards a wicker chair. "Sit down," he ordered.

She came forward and sat down.

"Cigarette?"

"No, thank you."

"Drink?"

"Please. Something long and cool."

He pulled the bell-rope and gave an order. Then he lay back on the long chair, lit a cigarette for himself and spoke.

"You're Miss Challis—right?"

"Emma Challis. I'm not related to Lady Grantly, but I like her very much and I felt . . ."

"—that she needed someone with her when she came out

here. You were quite right. But weren't you going back to England almost at once?"

"No. I came for three weeks. What's so awful is that this is my last day. I'm booked on a flight tomorrow. Everything has been going so well, and Lady Grantly seemed so happy and so settled that I didn't mind leaving her. And then this happened."

"May I know exactly what?"

"We noticed three tin trunks on our back veranda last night. We didn't know anything about them, and the maids said they didn't know anything either. But this morning, I heard . . . No, I smelled this terribly strong smell of cooking, and went to investigate, and saw this . . ." She paused and then went on more shakily. "It was horrible. The mother and the five children—not exactly ragged, but that sort of reach-me-down look. Huddled in one of the crates that the furniture had come in. They're enormous and—"

"I know. Go on."

"There was a sort of tension—the maids had that look of mulishness. . . . Well, they made it clear that they knew nothing about her. Then Alípio came. He's the—"

"The chauffeur. So?"

"He questioned the woman and then a sort of row blew up. I told Lady Grantly they were squatters, and of course they are, but there's something more in it. The woman's got a lost, frightened, hopeless sort of look."

"Did anyone mention the police?"

"Yes. The chauffeur did, but Lady Grantly wouldn't hear of it because the children were so thin and starved-looking."

A servant came out with a large frosted jug of fruit juice. Mr. Weybridge called him back as he was going away, and looked at Emma.

"I'm going to send Alípio away. I'll take you back in my car. That'll give you more time to talk. All right?"

"Yes."

The order was given and the servant went through the iron gate that led to the courtyard.

"How old are these children?" Mr. Weybridge asked.

"They go from nine down to about three."

"Any labels on the trunks?"

"Yes, but I didn't read them. Perhaps I should have."

"It would have helped."

"They were very old and battered and—"

"You didn't understand anything that was said?"

"Not a word. But the chauffeur and the maids were . . ."

"Well?"

"Hostile. That's the word I've been looking for. That's what's wrong. That's why I . . . well, I didn't exactly panic, but I was worried. I could have understood their being angry and wanting to get the woman off Lady Grantly's premises, but it was more than anger. It was something nastier. They—"

She stopped. He was on his feet, leaning over to pick up his glass and drain the contents.

"I'll go and put something on. Shan't be long," he said.

He was back within ten minutes, in a sport shirt and a pair of blue linen trousers. He led Emma out to the courtyard; Lady Grantly's car had vanished and his own stood in its place. He helped Emma in and started the car.

"Will you still be going back to England tomorrow?" he asked as they drove out onto the road.

"Yes. Unless this woman in the crate proves to be some kind of trouble-maker. My fiancé wasn't pleased when I came out and he'll be even less pleased if I don't go back on schedule."

"When's the wedding?"

"September. But we haven't found a house yet."

"London?"

"Yes, unfortunately."

"Where would you rather have a house?"

"Here," she said unguardedly. "Not seriously," she went on. "I've just been a bit bemused by all the colour. It's my first trip abroad, and it went to my head, I suppose."

"Not head. Senses. How long have you known Lady Grantly?"

"Hardly any time at all. I met her because my fiancé's father, who's my godfather, married her great-niece."

"I'll work that out some other time. She asked you to come out here with her?"

"She took it for granted."

"Why wasn't your fiancé pleased?"

"Because he considered she was capable of looking after herself. Up to a point, she is. After that point, no. What I was afraid of was people taking advantage of her. She's not silly, but she can't resist an appeal. When Senhor Tavares came to—"

"Augusto went to the house?"

"Yes."

"What in the world for?"

"He brought a portfolio with several of his own paintings, several he said were done by his pupils—and a picture of Lady Grantly's house." She paused to let Mr. Weybridge's mirth subside. "Does he go round getting pupils like that?"

"Was that what he was after?"

"That's what he got. Wednesday and Friday mornings."

"Perhaps he's hit on something profitable at last."

"Hasn't he got any money? He ought to have. I like his work—it looks to me as though it ought to sell."

"Some of it does, but not enough to feed and clothe him and keep that great crumbling house of his going. Half of it has already collapsed, to his great relief. Once the rest goes, he'll be a happy man."

"Can't he leave it before it falls down?"

"No. It's been a Tavares property from the year sixteen hundred and something. My mother tried to get his father to blow it up, but he was horrified. Sacred trust, he said. So poor Augusto's stuck with it, living in three rooms and letting the other forty or so die of damp. Did Lady Grantly want to take lessons in painting?"

"Not until he hinted at poverty."

"Morning lessons with lunch, you'll find—or she'll find. Now I can see why you shouted at me. You couldn't understand anyone turning away from an appeal. You and Lady Grantly are both obviously dedicated to the principle of helping people, while I'm equally enthusiastic about letting them help themselves. I can never understand how people like you—people with a friendly air—get through life."

"Why did all those clients you told me about go to you with their problems? Perhaps you've got a friendly air, too."

"Would you say I had?"

"Anything but. But then I yelled at you. If I hadn't, perhaps I would have seen your honeyed side."

"There is no honeyed side. The honey is what makes people stick. How does your fiancé deal with your instinct for protecting the weak—in this case, Lady Grantly?"

"I've told you. He didn't want me to come out. Of course, if I'd known you were living so close to her, I would have realized that she wouldn't need me. Mr. Weybridge is out.

Mr. Weybridge is still out. One of these days, an angry client might push you into your pool."

He did not reply. They were near the house, and they could see Lady Grantly on the terrace. She came to meet them.

"Emma, how clever of you to find Mr. Weybridge. Good morning, Mr. Weybridge. She's still here, poor creature. I've given her a mattress for the smallest children. Two of them are asleep. Do you know, they've come all the way from Mozambique. It's written on the trunk labels. I couldn't remember where that was at first, and then it came back to me—it's that island that belongs to France, which I passed once in the Caribbean."

"That was probably Martinique," he told her. "Mozambique is Portuguese and it's in, or rather is part of, Southeast Africa."

"Good heavens! Could she have come all that way with those poor little children?"

"If you'll show me where they are, we'll try to find out," he suggested.

Lady Grantly led the way. The little family in the crate looked more pathetic than ever. The mother, after one glance, looked away and went on with her preparations for a meal— as before, pieces of bread dropped into a watery-looking soup. Mr. Weybridge walked up to the crate and addressed her.

The two maids stood apart, saying nothing but following every word. Alípio stood beside Mr. Weybridge and once tried to put in a word, only to be very sharply silenced. Mr. Weybridge, leaning in a relaxed manner against the wall of the outhouse, continued to address the woman, and under his quiet handling, she dried her tears, came out of the crate, smoothed back her hair and answered his questions. At a certain stage in the conversation, she turned and produced from one of the tin trunks a soiled envelope out of which Mr. Weybridge drew some papers. He examined them and then apparently asked her permission to keep them. After a long, searching look into his eyes, she nodded, and he put the envelope and its contents into his wallet. Then he straightened and addressed Lady Grantly.

"That's all for the moment, I think," he said. "Shall we go into the house?"

He said no more until they were in the drawing room. He seemed thoughtful, but his face gave no clue to the nature of his thoughts.

"Would you agree," he asked Lady Grantly at last, "to allow me to find accommodations for the woman and her children? By which I mean would you agree to pay for it?"

"My dear Mr. Weybridge, how can you ask? Did you see those children's ribs? Where do you think you could find a place?"

"Not far from here. The artist who gives you painting lessons, Augusto Tavares, has a house—as I've just been telling Miss Challis—which is extremely large and which he hasn't the money to keep up. He only occupies a fraction of it, and I think it would be a good idea to house this family in his servants' quarters, which are empty."

"But you said the house was falling down," Emma protested.

"It won't fall down yet, and it'll only fall down by degrees. There's furniture, and there's wood for the gathering, there's a large kitchen with a good stove, and as the only person who looks after Augusto is an aged crone from the village, we might arrange that this woman cook for him. Would you agree to this?"

"Of course! But would Senhor Tavares agree?" Lady Grantly asked.

"He'll agree," Mr. Weybridge stated confidently. "I'll talk to him today."

"I'm most grateful to you," Lady Grantly said with relief. "And do forgive me—I haven't even offered you a drink. And please, Mr. Weybridge, do stay and have lunch, won't you?"

He hesitated. Emma thought he was framing a polite refusal, but to her surprise, he accepted.

"Thank you. I'd like to," he said. "But I'm afraid there's something which we shall have to discuss."

"Something to do with that poor woman?" Lady Grantly asked him.

"Yes."

"Why are you afraid? Is it something unpleasant?"

"Yes."

"Well, at least you're not going to tell me to send her away. I shouldn't have agreed to that."

His eyes rested on her speculatively, and Emma felt a prick of uneasiness; he seemed to be assessing just how much shock she could take.

"There wouldn't have been any question of sending her away," he said quietly. "You see, if these papers"—he touched the pocket which contained his wallet—"if these papers are in order, which I'm pretty certain they are, and if those children are who she claims them to be, then . . ."

He paused, and Emma's uneasiness deepened.

"Well, if the children are who she claims them to be, then what?" Lady Grantly asked.

"Then half this house belongs to them," said Mr. Weybridge.

Chapter
7

Lady Grantly was in bed. She had listened in silence to
Robert Weybridge as he recounted, briefly and swiftly, the
facts on which the claims of the children rested. She had
looked confused and shaken when he ended, but had insisted
that all she needed was a glass of sherry before going on to eat
a hearty meal. The drink had been left untouched and she
had agreed, towards the end of a barely tasted meal, to
Emma's suggestion of a rest. The younger maid, Lourdes,
revealing a strong maternal streak, undressed her and got
her into bed. Only when her head was on the pillow did Lady
Grantly admit that perhaps the heat had been a little too
much for her.

Emma drew the curtains and left her to recover. Over
coffee in the cool, shuttered drawing room, Robert filled in
for her the more disturbing details he had felt it wise to omit
when speaking to Lady Grantly.

The facts were simple enough. Two brothers, Manuel and
Duarte, had built and shared the house. They were constantly

quarrelling, and ten years ago, after a particularly bitter dispute, Duarte had packed his belongings and gone to Mozambique. Nothing had been heard of him until two years ago, when he went to visit a cousin and died while staying in his house. The cousin wrote to Manuel telling him the news, and in due course sent him the death certificate and other necessary papers for the purpose of identification. Nobody but Manuel had any claim to the property. The house became his and he registered it in his name. A short while later, he realized that foreigners were moving into the district and local farmers were growing rich by selling them houses and land. Manuel had no land, but he had a house. He went to Senhor Melo for advice, engaged an architect recommended by him, spent all the money he had on converting the house, sold it at a handsome profit and then proceeded to realize his dream of owning a farm in Angola.

But what neither Manuel nor anybody else had known was the fact that Duarte, shortly after arriving in Mozambique, had married. Nobody, not even the cousin in whose house he had died, had been told of the marriage. Now his wife had arrived in Portugal, and the papers in her possession proved that the marriage had taken place and that the children were his. As in Portugal there was no primogeniture, all five would inherit equally.

"So she's going to claim half the house?" Emma asked.

"No. At the moment she isn't going to claim anything. She came here simply because she couldn't make a living for herself and the children out in Mozambique. She knew nothing beyond the fact that in or near this village called Aldeia da Torre, near Sintra, her husband had owned half a house. She can read and write, but she didn't think of writing to Manuel. Or perhaps she preferred to come here and feel her way—her husband had probably told her about the quarrels, and she wasn't sure what sort of reception she'd get. She scraped together enough money for the fares, arrived in Lisbon, made her way first to Sintra and then to the village. There she made a few enquiries—and got a poor reception."

"Why?"

"Because the village is prospering due to the many foreigners who are living here, and Lady Grantly is already recognized as a fount of benevolence. Nobody in the village wants to see her claim to the house threatened, for their sakes as well as for hers. So they told the woman she was an imposter and ordered her to clear out."

"They might have believed that she was making false claims."

"They might, but I doubt it. Nobody could look at any one of those five children and doubt that Duarte was the father. I suppose what they doubted was their legitimacy; at least two of the village women have been living in hopes that Duarte would return one day and marry them. He liked women, Duarte did. So did Manuel. They usually went after the same one, and that was what all the quarrelling was about."

"So what happens now? You said she wouldn't claim."

"No, I didn't. I said that she wasn't thinking of claiming at the moment. She's a simple, ignorant peasant who has no idea, as yet, what's due to her. She can't think in terms of a claim, but someone might put her up to it, in which case a judge might rule that the contract of sale is null and void."

"Judge?"

"Of course. This is going to end up in the courts one day."

"But how can a judge say the contract's void? Everybody acted in good faith."

"What's that got to do with it?"

"If there's to be a case, it's only between Manuel and this woman."

"And the person who bought the house. What you've got to realize, and get Lady Grantly to realize when she's gotten over the shock, is that this matter will have to be dug out by the roots. It's that old business of wheels within wheels. Manuel registered the property in his own name—but the property wasn't his. That's the first thing that will have to be unscrambled. No, not the first. The first will be an investigation of the circumstances of Duarte's death. Then there's the little matter of proving the widow's matrimonial claims, so that the children can be declared legitimate. Then there'll be the little matter of finding out how Manuel's going to react. There's no question of his being able to pay out any money to his brother's widow; I know for a fact that everything he made out of the sale of this house went into the purchase of his farm in Angola. I can't see him selling out and hastening back here to do justice to the widow of a brother he didn't get on with. I'm thirty-five. I'll probably be sixty-five before we're through with all these tangles. And Lady Grantly will be dead."

"Do you know where Manuel's farm is?"

"Yes. We have his address at the office."

"Are you going to write to him?"

"Of course."

"And if he doesn't answer, then what?"

"We write again. And again. And then we get in touch with a lawyer over there and put him on to it. Then we . . . As I said, wheels within wheels. I'm sorry this had to come up just as you're leaving."

"Leaving? You don't imagine, do you, that I'm going to leave Lady Grantly in the state she's in?"

"You've got responsibilities in London, haven't you?"

"That's what my fiancé keeps saying. A week won't make any difference, will it?"

"Not knowing the state of your feelings, or his, I can't answer. I could make a guess, if you'd like me to."

"I wouldn't. Are you going in to the office this afternoon?"

"Yes. It's contrary to my usual practice, but I've got to get Milou on to looking up documents. We won't get very far until Melo gets back. In the meantime, I'll let those lawyers in London know what's happened, which means reopening the correspondence with some fatuous idiot who signs himself Delfont and who did nothing throughout the purchase negotiations but tell me what I should have done, and . . . What did you say?"

"I said I was engaged to him."

"What—Delfont?"

"Delmont."

"Nonsense."

"What's nonsense about it?"

"It can't be the same fellow. Gordon, Gilbert, something of that kind?"

"Gerald."

"That's the one. Is it his father you said was something to do with Lady Grantly's great-niece? She knows this Gerald?"

"Yes."

"And likes him? No. I remember her saying she didn't, the first time I took her out to see the house. Is that why she never mentions your engagement?"

"It's one of the reasons. The other is that she doesn't want me to leave Portugal."

"I'm only judging by his letters, but are you sure you want to marry a fellow who uses six words where one would do? A man, moreover, who thinks he knows more about Portuguese law than the lawyers practising it in Portugal? Have you given it serious thought?"

"Yes, I have."

"Does he talk like his letters?"

"No."

"Known him long?"

"All my life."

"Then there shouldn't be any nasty surprises," he conceded. "This hitch is going to upset him even more than it's upset Lady Grantly. The only thing that'll cheer him up will be the realization that he was correct in assuming that I didn't know my business."

There was silence for a time, and then Emma put a question. "Did you come to live out here because you had a house here?"

"No. I've always been quite certain, ever since I was very small, that Portugal was where I wanted to live. Perhaps having Portuguese blood has something to do with it, but I don't think so. I've never understood why people who reach the age of discretion shouldn't be able to choose their nationality as they can choose their religion. One can be naturalized, of course, but it's all a bit of a fuss. Some people are born flag-waggers, and some aren't. National anthems make me feel acutely embarrassed. So does all that my-country-'tis-of-thee business. My boyhood hero was Lord Byron, who fought not for a country but for a cause. My father was one of the last stalwarts who went round the British Empire keeping its remnants together; if he'd been a different kind of man, he would have lived in France after his retirement, because he loved France and thought it had all the beauty and history and culture that any man could want. But he couldn't see himself as an expatriate, and so he uttered all the usual platitudes about the delights of being in an English garden, and bought himself one—far too large, like the house that was attached to it—and tried to persuade my mother that they were living an ideal existence. She considered it pure hell, but it didn't last long; he hacked down too many trees and laid too many crazy pavements, and finished himself off a good ten years before he need have. She came out here after he died."

"To the house you're living in?"

"For a time. Then she went up to a quinta she owned near Oporto. I go there whenever I can."

"Did you ever practise law in England?"

"I was with a firm of lawyers for a couple of years in London, but I never felt at home. I needed this feeling I get so strongly every time I come back to Portugal—a good-earth feeling. Old shepherds sitting on stone walls watching a couple of dozen sheep, peasants gathering olives, stripping cork, harvesting grapes, following a Biblical type of plough. There's still rural life in England, but if you're a city dweller, you have to go a long way to find it. Here, it's within five minutes of any city. It's all round you, all the time. Industry's coming, but it hasn't taken over yet. I shall be dead, thank God, and perhaps my sons too, before this country loses its slow, lovely rhythm. You feel it too, which surprises me."

"I didn't mention rhythm. I said I didn't want to go away, and I don't, but that's because being out here has weakened my moral fiber."

"Oh, you have moral fiber? Could I put it to the proof?"

"No. If you'll take me into Sintra with you, I'll cancel my booking and send a telegram while you're in the office."

"Saying you're delayed?"

"Saying there's a claimant. Will you take me?"

"Of course."

"Then wait while I see how Lady Grantly is."

She was asleep. Emma, having peeked in, went to her room to change her dress. Then she telephoned to Mrs. Cooper, gave her a brief account of what had happened and asked her to come across in about an hour to see how Lady Grantly was feeling. Then she joined Robert.

They did not go directly to Sintra. They took a narrow, winding road that began at the village and trailed off, it seemed, into nowhere. Somewhere along its rutted length was an ancient pair of gateposts whose gate had long since vanished, and which now served only to mark the beginning of a once-noble drive. Along this Robert guided his car with care, following curves that were lit by the sun, now obscured beneath the deep shade of overhanging trees. He bumped over the ruts of the last bend and then stopped. In front of them Emma saw a house which he had already described to her—the house which belonged to Senhor Tavares.

Even in a state of decay, it was beautiful—but it was the setting which caught her imagination. While the house had been falling into ruin, nature had flourished and continued to grow and spread. The flower gardens were lost. Long grass, rushes, weeds, wild bushes, spreading creepers rioted almost to the long, beautiful windows. Ivy hid the cracks in the walls, moss covered the holes in the roof. Long tendrils of rosebushes lay across the stone terrace and the broad sweep of steps, tripping Robert and Emma as they walked towards the one window which was open. Looking round as she reached the top of the steps, she could see in the distance a series of collapsed stone walls; there were glimpses of marble statues, whole or mutilated, and a fountain with a cracked basin.

"What a terrible pity," she murmured. "Couldn't they have done anything to keep it . . . alive?"

"Of course they could." He bent to disentagle the weeds that were clinging to his trousers. "They could have employed armies of gardeners. They could have installed heating to keep the damp at bay. They could have engaged busy little maids and busy big footmen. They could have kept on the coachman and kept up the carriages—if they'd had the money. But they hadn't and so they couldn't and so they didn't. Augusto's grandfather was the last occupant who kept up any state. When he died, there was a family conclave and Augusto's father was elected to keep the sacred flame alight. When he died, all he left to Augusto was the furniture and the responsibility for finding the money to keep the place going. Well, you can look round and draw your own conclusions. Let's go inside." He raised his voice to a yell. "Hey, Augusto!"

Round the corner of the house came Senhor Tavares, a strange figure clad in a pair of creased pajamas. When he saw Emma, he gave a moan of embarrassment and vanished.

"Go inside, go inside, go inside," he called. "I will soon come to you."

Robert led Emma through empty, echoing rooms smelling of damp, and along corridors whose walls still bore the imprints of the pictures that had once hung on them. Then he opened the door of a room which faced a moss-covered terrace. It was furnished as a combination of study and studio; in one corner was an unmade bed. Raising his voice once more, Robert summoned the sole servant, a black-clad old woman who at sight of him gave voice to a stream of benedictions followed by cackling reminiscences. When Robert had responded to these, he asked for coffee for three.

Three? But Senhor Tavares, she explained, had only just finished his breakfast.

"Then for two."

As she departed, Senhor Tavares came in looking spruce and shaven. They talked Portuguese; it would be good, Robert said, for Emma to get some practise.

She followed most of what was said, assisted by the fact that she knew what Robert had come to ask. Senhor Tavares, at first lukewarm, gradually perceived the advantages of the plan, and ended by agreeing to allocate three rooms to Duarte's widow and her five children. The rooms, which they chose together, were on the ground floor and adjoined the vast kitchen; they also gave access to the garden.

"Well, what do you think, Emma?" Robert asked at last, reverting to English.

"Does she have to cook in that enormous fireplace?"

"Where else? There's enough wood out in that wilderness to last for a hundred years. I'll send someone along with a saw, and soon you'll see all the children sitting round, or perhaps in, the fireplace, holding hot bowls of soup."

"How about furniture?"

"That is difficult," Augusto declared. "Robert cannot expect that I should give them my fine furniture which my father especially—"

"Augusto, talk sense," Robert broke in. "Is there one single piece in any of those rooms upstairs that isn't riddled with worms? Emma's not going to select the period stuff, as Lady Grantly would undoubtedly have done; she'll choose good, solid, worm-eaten chairs and tables and beds from the staff quarters at the top of the house. And now let's go back to your studio and talk money."

"Ah, money," murmured Augusto, leading the way. "Money, money . . ."

The financial part of the transaction concluded, Robert telephoned to Lady Grantly's house and spoke to Alípio. He was to bring the woman and her children, he said, to the house of Senhor Tavares and go back for their luggage.

Emma was not long in choosing the furniture; it was merely a matter of selecting those pieces which the worms had liked least.

"While I'm at it," Robert said, when they had left Senhor Tavares and were on their way to Sintra, "I'll send a truck to cart away that furniture crate. Otherwise you'll wake up one morning and find it full of gypsies."

He was at the office until six o'clock. Emma spent the last part of the waiting period writing a letter to Gerald, seated at the table in Senhor Melo's waiting room, surrounded by the minature boots and shoes. Robert came in as she was sealing the envelope.

"Sorry to have kept you so long."

"I've been writing a letter."

"To your fiancé? So have I. I hope he'll be able to unsnarl the unhappy facts. Would you like to bet he'll blame it all on me?"

"No."

"Will you come back to my house and endure a bit more waiting while I have a shower? Then I'll take you back, and if Lady Grantly's up to it, I'll give her a report. There's nothing new. Duarte didn't leave a will; his widow was pretty certain that he never made one, and I've just been going through the stuff that the notary in Mozambique sent to us when Manuel was clearing things up after Duarte's death."

"Would a will have made things easier?"

"I don't know what he would have put into it. I prefer things the way they are. Ready?"

"Yes." She followed him out to the car. "But why a shower? Why not a swim? I can't think of anything I'd like more than to get into that pool—or any pool. If it's too much trouble to run me home to fetch my swimsuit, there's a rather nice one in a shop window I've been looking at."

He drove her to the shop and she bought the wisp of green material which Robert declared to be all straps and no body. Nothing in her life had ever given her such keen pleasure as the feel of the water on her overheated body. Nothing would have given her more pleasure than to lie on one of the chairs and have a drink and listen to Robert's deep, unhurried tones —but Lady Grantly was on her mind.

When they got to her house, she was still in her room, but not in bed. Wearing a black satin kimono lavishly decorated with dragons, she was seated on a chair in her room, and on the edge of another chair was Mrs. Cooper, ready to spring up and supply anything that was needed.

"Emma, is that you?"

"Yes." Emma entered the room and bent to kiss the soft cheek. "Who gave you permission to get up?"

"She wouldn't stay in bed," Mrs. Cooper stated with patent disapproval. " 'I'm not ill,' she said. 'You've 'ad a bad shock,' I said. 'And I've got over it now,' she said."

"And so I have," said Lady Grantly. "And it wasn't a shock—it was that rather overpowering heat. I can bear it quite well when there's a nice breeze, as there is now. Is that Mr. Weybridge I can hear talking to Mr. Cooper?"

"Yes."

"Bring him in here, please. I'd like to thank him."

Robert hovered on the threshold and then, asked to report on his findings at the office, advanced and took a seat on the bed.

"Nothing much," he said. "I told Emma that this is going to take a very long time."

"I've been thinking about it, Mr. Weybridge. You see—"

"Would you mind calling me Robert?"

"I should very much prefer to. Thank you. Well, Robert, I've had time to think about this little complication. I've had a very good idea and I'd like to know what you think of it. That poor woman, you say, may be entitled, on behalf of her children, to half a share of this house. Well, if the man I bought it from—her brother-in-law—gives any sign of behaving badly and not replying to letters and so on, why shouldn't I ask you to make a fair price for her share, and give it to her?"

He assumed a grave air and appeared to consider this proposal.

"You have a very kind heart, Lady Grantly," he said at last, "but the suggestion isn't really workable."

"Why not? Justice must be done. If the man who sold the house to me won't meet his obligations, am I to let this poor creature—"

"Just a moment. She is, for the moment, very happy. Emma and I have installed her in Augusto Tavares's house, and as soon as you've got over this little touch of heat, we'll take you there and show you how well the arrangement is going to work."

"But it's purely temporary."

"In this country, temporary is a very long word."

"Why can't I, as it were, pay her compensation?"

"It would be very difficult to assess the value of her claim. She—"

"Well, it wouldn't be half of what I paid for the house, because it wasn't her husband who spent so much money doing it up. She's entitled, I would have said, to half the value that the house had when her husband went away and left it."

"Plus whatever a judge would estimate as additional by reason of the sharp increase in the value of land and property in this part of Portugal since her husband went to Mozambique."

"You're making it sound complicated again," Lady Grantly complained. "I had got it so nice and simple."

"If I could simplify it, I would. But it's really an almost inextricable tangle, and I'd like you to believe me when I say that it can't be settled for months. Years."

"*Years?*"

"It would be a very long process even if Manuel were still living in Portugal. As he's out in the blue some hundred miles from Luanda, dealing with him is going to be difficult, even if he proves cooperative."

"Is that poor woman going to have to wait years?"

"It won't seem like years. She's got a home and the children have got a lovely jungle to play in. She's also got a job and—"

"She must be paid for it, Robert. This I insist on. I won't hear of any other arrangement. If Senhor Tavares considers that the accommodation he's giving her is worth more than the service she's giving him, I shall pay the difference. And

I shall of course see that the children are provided for. That, at least, I hope you'll be able to arrange without delay?"

He said that he would, and she asked him to go and see that Mr. Cooper had a drink. He poured beer for Mr. Cooper, whiskey for himself, tonic water for Lady Grantly, tomato juice for Mrs. Cooper, and was just handing Emma her sherry when the telephone rang and a maid came in to tell her that there was a call for her from England.

It was unfortunate that the house was so small and the telephone on a table in the hall, close to the door of the drawing room. It was unfortunate, too, that it was a very bad line. Most unfortunate of all was Gerald's mood.

"Hello. Hello. May I speak to Miss Challis, please. C-h-a-l-l-i-s. *Je veux parler* . . . Hello. May I—"

"I'm speaking, Gerald. Hello? Gerald, it's—"

"Emma, is that you?"

"Yes."

"Speak up, will you? I can't hear a word. Is that you, Emma?"

"Yes. Did you get—"

"Blast this line, I can't hear a word. Hello, hello, *hello!* Will you please let me—"

"I'm *speaking*."

"They cut us off. Is that you?"

"Yes."

"I've just got your telegram. What the hell is it all about?"

"I told you in the telegram. There's a—"

"Hello, hello. Blast it, they've cut us off again. Are you there?"

"Yes."

"I've just got your telegram. I don't know what's happening out there, but it's nothing whatever to do with you.

You've got to come back as planned, do you hear? You've . . . Hello, hello."

"I'm *listening*."

"Is that you?"

"*Yes.*"

"I don't understand what's going on, but you've got to come back. Can you hear me?"

"Yes. I told you in my telegram—"

"Yes, I got it. Can you hear? I got your telegram. Hello, hello . . ."

She replaced the receiver, drew a deep breath and discovered that the Coopers had left. She went back to Lady Grantly's room and Robert brought in her sherry.

"Sorry about all the shouting," she apologized. "Bad line."

"I didn't know you'd sent him a telegram," Lady Grantly said.

"Well, I did. I told him I was staying on."

"And he insists on your going home at once, of course?"

Emma smiled. "Yes. But Robert's written him a letter explaining everything and telling him the heat's been worrying you. I wrote to him too, telling him I was going to stay with you until you felt better."

"I shan't feel better until this case is settled, and Robert says that'll be years. So I'm not going to think about it any more. I'm just going on as before. I shall look after the woman and her children and I shall leave Robert to deal with all the other matters. And I shall get on with my painting. Senhor Tavares is very pleased with my work. I should be completely happy if you'd only give up this silly idea of marrying Gerald Delmont. Just because she knew him when she was a little girl is no reason for marrying him, is it, Robert?"

"I wouldn't have said so. It's her kind heart. People take advantage."

"They *do*, Robert, they *do*. But what can I do about that?"

"In this country, they have one word of advice for all troubles, large or small: *Paciencia*. It means fifty per cent patience and the rest resignation. So . . . *paciencia*."

"I don't see any point in being patient if I'm merely going to be resigned at the end of it. I shall be quite patient if I know that everything's going to be all right in the end," Lady Grantly declared. "Why don't you take Emma out to dinner?"

"Some other time," Emma said. "I'm going to stay with you tonight."

"I'm going into the office again tomorrow," Robert told her. "Coming?"

"Yes, go," urged Lady Grantly. "I shall be busy painting. It isn't Senhor Tavares's day, but he said he would come. I should like him to stay and have lunch with me, but perhaps now that he's got a woman to cook properly for him, he won't want to."

"He will want to," Robert prophesied, and took his leave.

Emma walked out to the car with him.

"She's looking better," he said. "Why not change your mind and come out with me?"

"Because she's not looking as well as she should."

"Then I'll pick you up tomorrow morning just before ten. I think—"

He stopped. He was searching his pockets. Emma watched him, and presently apprehension began to creep over her.

"You haven't . . . lost anything?" she asked.

"No. Yes, I have. My cigarette case. I remember putting it down on that small table in the drawing room. I'll go and get it."

It was not on the table. It was not in the drawing room. The maids helped in the search, and Lady Grantly watched through the open door of her room. Robert went outside again, and Emma followed him and watched him as he searched the floor of the car.

"I think I know where it is," she said at last.

He straightened and turned to stare at her. "Oh, you do? Then why on earth didn't you say so?"

"Because I'm not sure. But I think . . . well, I'm almost sure Mr. Cooper has got it."

"Mr. *Cooper?* What would Mr. Cooper want with . . . Look, how about explaining?"

"You'll get it back. All I have to do is to go and see Mrs. Cooper tomorrow and . . ."

Under his astonished gaze, her voice faltered and died.

There was a pause. Then Robert spoke in a dazed voice. "Perhaps I'm fuddled after that sixteenth of an inch of whiskey, but do I understand you to say that your neighbour has walked off with my cigarette case?"

"Perhaps. I mean, I think so. It was the shock, the doctor said. One minute, they were in Silver Street, and the next minute, he had no job, no interest in life and—"

"Will my cigarette case give him an interest in life?"

"It's a . . . he's a medical case."

"Medical or criminal?"

"I've just told you—it was the shock."

"Then he's got another one coming. I'm going to—"

"No, you're not. I've already told you—why don't you listen? I'll get it back for you tomorrow. He can't help it. It's because he was so poor and suddenly became rich."

"Oh, that was the shock?"

"If you can't be more sympathetic about it, would you mind going home?"

"Mind? I can't get away fast enough. Where are my studs? Oh, good! I'm still wearing them."

"Will you please go away?"

"Certainly. Say good night nicely."

Before she could stop him, he had taken her in a firm embrace and placed his lips on hers.

"It's the shock," he explained, releasing her. "And incidentally, may I be allowed to remark that for a girl who's engaged, you're considerably out of practise? See you tomorrow."

She stood watching his car out of sight.

Chapter 8

Lady Grantly announced next day that she was better. Emma thought that she still looked shaken, but could not prevent her from getting up to have her painting lesson. Clad in a garment that might be labelled tea gown, housecoat or caftan, she prepared to receive the master. His method of teaching seemed odd to Emma, but it also seemed effective. He placed Lady Grantly before her easel at one of the windows of the drawing room, and put his own easel slightly behind hers, so that he could see her work, while his own was out of her sight. The two then proceeded to paint the view which, as they were regarding it from the same angle, might be supposed when transferred to canvas to have certain similarities. But Emma, looking at the previous lesson's productions, realized the truth of the maxim about the eye of the beholder, for Senhor Tavares had created a wild seascape while Lady Grantly had painted a vivid green lawn, scarlet blobs to represent flowers and a wavy blue line to indicate the sea beyond.

She wandered out onto the terrace to wait for Robert. She knew that the morning would only begin for her when she saw him getting out of his car and coming towards her—but after lying awake last night, she had taken a firm resolution which in the clear light of day she had confirmed: to avoid all mind-searching, or heart-searching. She was happy. For the moment, let that suffice.

She told Robert as they drove away that she wished the idea of painting lessons had originated in her mind and not in Senhor Tavares's.

"Why didn't I think of it? It's given her such pleasure, and a new interest."

"Augusto only thought of it because he was thinking of the financial angle. Would you mind if we drove by his house to see how the family's settling down? I've brought my camera and I'd like to take a snap or two."

They passed Augusto in the village and stopped to have a word with him.

"Don't let Lady Grantly get tired," Emma requested. "She says she's feeling all right, but she doesn't look—"

"How can she tire, doing what gives her such pleasure?" he wanted to know. "To sit quietly and paint, without speaking except to ask for my advice, without moving except to have perhaps some coffee—is this tiring?"

"You must curb her creativity," Robert said. "How often have you told me that painting—"

"Now you are going to make jokes," broke in Augusto.

"No, he's not," Emma said. "He's going to turn the car and take you the rest of the way to Lady Grantly's house."

"Thank you, no. To sit in the front," he explained, "would for three people be uncomfortable. And to sit in the back, even for one person, even if Robert did not also put dogs inside with the passengers, this is also uncomfortable. I will walk and try to remember that it is good for my health. Goodbye."

His garden, when Robert and Emma reached it, looked as wild as ever, but the brooding silence which had met them yesterday was broken by the shouts of the children playing in the wilderness. And the house, though as ruinous, no longer looked forlorn. The door of the kitchen stood open, garments fluttered on a clothesline, and the mother of the children was in the act of hanging up yet another of Augusto's shirts. As Robert and Emma approached, she smiled; it was a grave, slow smile of utter content, and it gave the last touch to a dark beauty that Emma had glimpsed in the depths of the furniture crate. Glossy hair neatly tied, black garments whipped by the wind round a still-lovely figure, a dark, smooth skin and black, beautiful eyes. Robert was taking his camera out of the car.

"Good morning, Maria. Everything going well?"

Everything, she said, was going very well.

"Call those children, will you? I want to take a few snaps of them."

They came in a rush and gathered round their mother and posed with an assurance that contrasted sharply with their hapless look in the crate. Robert removed the first snapshot from his camera, examined it and passed it round and allowed the children to keep it. The next two—one a family group and the other of Maria alone—he kept. With some instructions about stores and money, he left the family standing and waving, and drove Emma to Sintra. He dropped her in the shopping district and she made some purchases and then walked to the office, to find Robert and Milou and two clerks bent over a desk that was littered with a bewildering array of documents. Robert glanced up briefly.

"Shan't be long. Sit down."

She took a chair by the window. The view was beautiful, but it was at the figures in the room that she looked—the dark faces, Robert's as dark as any, the thin, brown fingers pointing, the move to push aside one set of papers and examine the next. The sun grew too hot and she moved away from the window, and Robert straightened and looked at his watch.

"Time to stop." He stretched and yawned. "Given a choice, I'd rather work forwards than backwards. Especially in this little snarl-up. The more we dig, the less I like it. All right, Milou, you can put them all away."

"Will you be coming in this afternoon, Mr. Weybridge?"

"Not if I can help it. Am I needed?"

"I don't think so. There's nothing you can do until Jorge and Paulo have looked over the land registration papers. We'll have them ready for you tomorrow."

"Good. Thanks. Ready, Emma? Would you mind," he asked her as they went out to the car, "if we made a detour on the way back?"

"As long as I'm sitting in front, you can fill the back with as much stuff as you like."

"When are you going to forget that?"

"Never. Suppose that fish had been a live lobster?"

"Well, it's nothing like that this time. I'm going to collect a present for Lady Grantly."

"What sort of present?"

"You'll see."

He drove along several very steep streets and at last went

through a wide gateway and stopped before a house almost smothered in purple bougainvillia.

"Francisco!" he yelled.

From an upper window a head was thrust out and a young man called in reply.

"Roberto! *Vou ja.*"

A few moments later, he came down the steps carrying a puppy. It wriggled frantically in his arms until he transferred it to Robert's, when it stopped wriggling and licked Robert's face.

"Oh, he's darling! Let me have him," Emma begged.

"He will jump out," Francisco warned in uncertain English. "Please, will you come inside?"

"Thanks, no," Robert answered. "I think we'd better get back and give this animal to its new owner. Emma, Francisco's a distant cousin of mine. Say goodbye and I'll bring you over one day to meet the rest of his family."

Emma said goodbye, not only to Francisco but also to his three younger sisters, two younger brothers and one of his aunts, all of whom declared that they had come out to take a farewell look at the puppy.

"But their object," Robert explained on the way home, "was to take a look at you. They think it's time I married and settled down. Why couldn't you have kept your engagement ring out of sight?"

"Hasn't Francisco got any sisters of marriageable age?"

"Not any more. I let them slip through my grasp."

"That reminds me." She opened her bag. "Your cigarette case."

He took it and slipped it into his pocket. "Thanks. What's the procedure for the recovery of stolen property?"

"Mrs. Cooper just gives the things back. He doesn't miss them."

"It's just done for the hell of it—is that it?"

"Yes. Poor Mr. Cooper."

"Poor Mrs. Cooper. Shall we have lunch by the pool?"

"I'd like to, but I won't. Augusto will go on and on and—"

"He'll stop the moment his stomach tells him to, and that'll be well before lunch time. Then she'll ask him to stay. Maybe she'll ask me, too."

"Why didn't you ever arrange an exhibition of his work and make him famous?"

"My mother tried—that is, she tried to arrange an exhibition. But he wouldn't play. He made several excuses, and at last she realized that he couldn't face the agony of watching people looking at his pictures and then going away without buying them."

"Why don't you try him again? Lady Grantly would go round sticking SOLD on every single exhibit. She's going to adore this puppy. What's his name?"

"It's long and tongue-twisting; I thought I'd let her choose one."

Her pleasure and gratitude were boundless. The puppy, sensing that he had come home, gave her all his attention and answered her exclamations with ecstatic yelps.

"Don't spoil him, or I'll take him away again. And don't feed him between meals. And don't let him yap," Robert directed. "And don't stop him if he wants to chase cats; you'll make him feel frustrated."

"I shall look after him like a mother. What's his name?"

"You're to choose one," Emma told her.

"Does it have to be a Portuguese name?"

"Of course," said Robert. "You must address him exclusively in Portuguese."

"Now you're being absurd—isn't he, Senhor Tavares?"

"He likes to play these jokes," Augusto explained. "The little dog has good lines. You must call him a name that is not shameful, like some names the English call their dogs, names like Whiskers or even Sausage. This I do not like. Once I asked them to call a dog Raul, and they did, but then they were angry because when he was called and they had to say his name many times, they said it sounded like barking. And now look, this little dog has made a mistake on the terrace, and there is a river. This means you must call him Tejo, which is the river Tagus. Do you like that name?"

Lady Grantly tried it and said she liked it very much. So the puppy was called Tejo.

"Are you staying to lunch?" she asked Robert. "Senhor Tavares is going to stay."

"Is that an invitation? If it is, I accept with pleasure."

"Good. Emma, tell them to lay another place, will you? Are those papers and things you've been looking at in order, Robert?"

"Perfect order, I fear."

"Then if they're in order, why can't I just admit that—"

"Lady Grantly, *please!*"

"Oh, very well. But it does seem to me ridiculous that if those little children are, in fact, entitled to something, they should have to wait years and years before getting it. You said yourself it might be when I'm dead, so—"

"My dear Lady Grantly, I—"

"Well, you insinuated it. So why can't I make a will leaving half the house to Emma and the other half to the children, and then there won't be the slightest complication. If I had my way, people would be able to do the right thing *because* it's the right thing, and not because the law, after dragging on for years, tells them it's the right thing at last, which is what one knew all along without needing the opinion of judges and so on."

"The children are very happy," Robert told her. "As soon as the weather's a bit cooler, I'll drive you over to Augusto's house and you shall see for yourself."

"*Are* they happy, Senhor Tavares?" she asked.

"They make much noise, madam, but it is not crying noise. Yes, I think that they are very happy. I, too, am happy. Maria is a very good cook. Yesterday she made for my dinner a soup and some fish and some *bifes* such as I have not eaten except at the homes of others. And my clothes are now taken away to be washed; I do not have to ask, as before. I have . . . No, Robert. It is forbidden to take off the cloths which I have spread over the painting. This I will not allow until the pictures are finished. A pupil's work is the business only of the master."

"Quite right, Senhor Tavares," Lady Grantly said approvingly. "People make unkind remarks."

"And then the inspiration of the artist is gone—pouf!—like that," Senhor Tavares said.

"Robert, will you see to the drinks?" Lady Grantly asked. "I think a little chilled white port would do me good."

Senhor Tavares thought that it would do him good, too. His appetite at lunch was enormous, which pleased Lady Grantly but disappointed Tejo, who hovered hopefully by his chair throughout the meal.

When they were drinking coffee in the drawing room, Robert had a suggestion to make. "Would you think it a good idea, Lady Grantly, to transfer the painting lessons to my garden until the weather cools down a bit? It's never too hot near the pool, and you'd get a new view to paint."

"That's most kind of you, Robert. I should like that very much. Isn't it a good idea, Senhor Tavares?"

"It will be cooler, yes. But I must say to Robert that we do not paint the same view every time. This room has four windows, and from each is a different outlook, even if only a little different."

"I've got a commission for you," Robert said. "To paint Emma in her new swimsuit. It's green. You'll need ninety-nine and three-quarters per cent flesh tint and the rest green."

"Now *that*," Lady Grantly said, "is a splendid idea, but I hope that you will allow me to commission the artist. Senhor Tavares, will you do it for me?"

He said that it would give him the greatest pleasure, and then said that it was time for him to go.

"Emma, ask them to tell Alípio—" began Lady Grantly.

"I'll take Augusto," Robert broke in. "I'm taking Emma for a swim at my house and we can drop him on the way."

"Thank you. The Coopers have asked Emma and myself to dinner tomorrow, and they included you, Robert. Can you accept?"

"May I let you know when I've looked at my little book? I rather think I'm already dining out."

"A very transparent excuse," Emma commented, when they had dropped Senhor Tavares.

"Why do I have to dine with the Coopers, for God's sake? It wasn't even a direct invitation."

"They didn't want to risk being told that you were already dining out."

"Would that surprise them—with only a day's notice?"

"No. It would only hurt them, that's all. They're shy. And they're lonely."

"I have to dine with every shy, lonely person who cares to invite me?"

"Only when they happen to be your clients."

"All right. I'll be kind. I'll try to make them less shy and lonely. But if they put on a single one of their daughter's records, I'll make another transparent excuse, and go home. So that's settled. The next thing is that I don't care who pays Augusto for the painting he's going to do of you, but I'm going to have it—is that clear?"

"I'll tell Lady Grantly."

"Good. Seriously, Emma, do you know what a lovely body you've got?"

"I'll take a new look at it when I'm getting into my swim-suit."

"Where shall we have dinner? I know three wonderful places. One's beside the sea, the other's in a pine wood and the third's underground—nice and cool. *Fados*. Want to hear *fados*?"

"Yes."

"Then what we'll do is dine by the sea and then drive into Lisbon at midnight and listen to *fados*. Sad, and haunting. Do you want to be sad and haunted?"

"Yes."

"Are you willing to be made sad and haunted by me?"

"Yes."

"When I take you out tonight, will you promise to be in the yes-mood you're in now?"

"Yes. No."

"Good."

"I said no."

"You said yes first. If a woman says yes first, what does it matter what she says next?"

"You can't take advantage of a woman who's under the influence. Of drink or drugs or anything else. I'd like to make it clear that this country has had a very peculiar effect on me."

"You haven't seen this country. You haven't seen the snow on the Estrela mountains. You haven't seen the lovely, quiet waters near Aveiro. You haven't seen the woods of Bussaco. You haven't seen Tomar, or Braga. You haven't driven across the mountains of the moon to Chaves."

"I told you that being out here had gone to my head. You said no, to my senses. What's seeing got to do with senses? Do you realize that never in my life, until I came here, had I seen hibiscus or oleander or magnolia? That's all I needed to see. I go out into the garden in the morning and close my eyes and just *feel* all that loveliness round me. I want to cry at night because I've realized for the first time how much of the world's beauties I've missed."

"Will you cry tonight?"

He had stopped the car in the courtyard she now knew so well. She turned to look at him.

"Cry? That depends on you, doesn't it?" she asked. "You can't expect me to be sad and haunted without crying, can you?"

He made no reply. He took her into the house, to a room on the ground floor which was lined with bookshelves and furnished with tables which were covered with photographs. He showed them to her—his father, his mother, himself at all stages—schoolboy, youth, man. He took her round the house, upstairs and down, and then left her to change and joined her at the pool and dived with her into the cool water. He changed at dusk into a suit and drove her to Lady Grantly's and waited until she had put on a dress suitable for the evening, and then they said good night to Lady Grantly and drove away together. And though the evening might haunt her, she knew, as she lay her head on her pillow that night, or near dawn the next morning, that there had been no sadness in it.

Chapter
9

Three of them—Lady Grantly, Emma and Robert—walked over to the Coopers for dinner after a preliminary drink at Lady Grantly's house. It was the hottest evening there had been since the heat wave began, but they sat down to soup with dumplings, a steak and kidney pudding and an apple tart. After this there was nothing to do but sit in the garden and try to recover enough energy for the walk home. Robert, after saying good night to Lady Grantly and walking with Emma to his car, discovered that in spite of the utmost vigilance, he had lost his fountain pen.

"Blast him," he muttered, giving up the search through his pockets and on the floor of the car, "I didn't take my eyes off him once."

"I'll get it back for you."

"You'll never be able to restore my digestion. I feel like a kangaroo with turbulent twins. Are you going to say good night properly?"

"No."

"Then I will," he said, and did so.

She went slowly into the house, switched off the terrace lights and walked into her room, heavy with food, drugged with happiness. Somewhere, she remembered hazily, as she got into bed, there was another country where people bustled about and looked for houses and kept abreast of current affairs. Here there were flowers, flowers, flowers and . . . and what else? Dogs that barked all night in the village, old women with their heads tied up in black shawls, and a heat haze that shimmered over everything and sharpened her senses but had a strangely paralyzing effect on her brain. She must remember tomorrow, or some time, to answer those two telegrams, those two very angry telegrams from Gerald asking when he might expect her. Expect her to . . . to what? She must answer tomorrow, or some time, his letter, irate to the point of abusiveness. Why did people get angry? Why were people so impatient? Where was the need for hurry? This case—hadn't Robert said so?—would take years, and years . . . and . . . years. . . .

By morning, she had forgotten everything but the fact that this was the day that had been chosen for the painting lesson by the pool. Visiting Lady Grantly in her room after breakfast, she found her selecting an outfit that would be suitable not only for the heat of the day, but also for the coolness of Robert's garden, the paw marks of the puppy, paint stains and the splashes from the pool.

"A smock is what I need, Emma. Why haven't I got a smock? I suppose because I've never needed one until now. What I *have* got, though, is that grey suit with the tunic top. If I just slipped the tunic part over a dress, it would look quite right, don't you agree?"

"You're sure you're not going to get too tired?"

"Of course not. I never felt better. Robert is such a *thought-ful* man, and so kind! How lucky that the other lawyer was away, so that we had to have Robert. He admires you very much, Emma, do you know that? I've watched him watching you. Last night, he scarcely took his eyes off you."

Which was why he lost his fountain pen, Emma reflected, and wondered when there would be an appropriate moment in which to explain Mr. Cooper's complaint. As far as she knew, he had never taken anything belonging to Lady Grantly, but that was possibly because she didn't carry cigarette cases or pens or pencils, and seldom troubled to take a handbag unless she was going on a shopping expedition.

"Can I help you to dress?" she asked.

"No. Would you send Lourdes in? She's very clever at lady's-maiding me. Oh, Emma, how lucky I am to be so happy here, with such nice maids. If only you wouldn't insist on marrying that man—especially with a man like Robert here, so different, so much more kind and so much, much more charming! I wish I could make you reconsider."

"Don't try," Emma said, and something in the tone made Lady Grantly turn and stare at her. At the look on Emma's face, she advanced a few steps and then paused.

"I've hurt you," she said slowly. "I'm sorry. I didn't mean to upset you in any way. All I want is your happiness—you know that, don't you?"

"Yes, I know." Emma took one of her hands and held it. "And I know how you feel about Gerald. All I want you to do is . . . not to say anything. Just leave it. Just leave everything . . . as it is."

"Couldn't I put it to the cards? The cards would—"

"No." She paused to steady her voice. "It's difficult to put this into words, but I'd like to be left to work things out for myself. I don't know whether I really want to marry Gerald or not. I've been too confused, since I came out here, to think clearly. But what I do know is that I don't want to make any decisions in the state of mind I'm in now. I wanted to get married. After thinking it over at a time when I could think clearly, I decided to marry Gerald. I had two terrible years in London when I was absolutely and utterly alone, and I learned then what a home and a background, what security and a husband who loved you, what someone to care for you and look after you could mean. I know how charming Robert is, but neither you nor I know anything about him, and if we did, we'd find that the fors and the againsts added up pretty much as they do in the case of Gerald. The only advantage Robert has is his setting. He's a part of all this sunshine that's got into my eyes. I'm not seeing clearly and I'm not thinking clearly, and now that you're . . . now that you're not feeling the heat so much, I want to pull myself together and get back where I belong. Where I think I belong."

"You can't live for the rest of your life in London."

"Eight or nine million people are doing just that. I'll make one more."

"He isn't good enough for you, Emma. But I've upset you, and I won't do it again. I love you, but your life is your own, and even if I think you're going to make a mess of it, I haven't any right to stop you. Kiss me. There. Now I won't say another word about Gerald Delmont, except to point out that he isn't half the man Robert is. You'll never meet anyone nicer or more suited to you than Robert. If you don't know much about him, it'll be all the more fun finding out when you're married. I was warned that Hamish had seduced every woman in every country he had been in, but I married him and we were very happy—oh, so happy! As happy and as gay and as faithful as you and Robert could be if—"

"You said you wouldn't."

"I know. I'm sorry. Go and send me Lourdes and I'll get dressed and try to enjoy you while I have you, without thinking of that— Well, send Lourdes to me."

Emma sent her. Her mind was more confused than ever, but one thing that Lady Grantly had said remained with her and seemed to her to be reasonable: to enjoy the present, to leave the future to take care of itself.

They drove to the pool—she and Lady Grantly and Augusto, for whom they called on the way there. The two dogs, after a brief inspection, decided that Tejo was harmless. Emma and Robert bathed. Augusto set up the two easels— but the setting, scenically perfect, had a quality which made for indolence rather than industry. The two artists very soon laid aside their brushes. The dogs dozed. Robert and Emma got out of the pool and lay side by side in the sun.

"Isn't this lovely?" Lady Grantly murmured, from her long, cushioned chair. "When I think of all the years I wasted not being here, I could weep. I could—"

She paused. Senhor Tavares had emerged from the house in his bathing attire, a sight to make anyone pause.

"Are you going to swim?" she asked him.

"Swim? No, madam. This I cannot do. But I shall stand in the water to cool myself. It is very refreshing. Is also very healthy."

The servants brought out lunch. Augusto hurried out of the pool, dressed and came out to eat as much as he could. He talked of the five children, and Lady Grantly wrote down their names to help her to remember them. She showed Robert the list: Peeper, Noonoo, Gargoo, Leaner, Meaner.

Robert returned the paper with the spelling corrected to Pipa, Nuno, Gago, Adelina and Guilhermina. She put beside their names a rough approximation of their ages and sizes, and said that she planned to equip them with shoes and shirts and dresses. In case this should rouse the envy of the village mothers, she was going to buy shoes and shirts and dresses for the village children, too.

"I shall do it tomorrow, for my birthday," she ended.

"Tomorrow's Saint Anthony's Day," Robert told her. "I'll take you to see the fires. That'll be a nice birthday treat."

"What fires?" Emma asked.

"The children light fires on the ground and join hands and jump over them. Perhaps I shouldn't have suggested taking Lady Grantly—you can't really enjoy the sight until it's properly dark."

"You shall certainly take me," Lady Grantly said.

"No, I shall be the one," called Augusto from the other side of the pool, where he had gone to work on his painting of Emma. "I am the one who is Portuguese; it is for me to explain our customs."

"Then we shall all have dinner together," Lady Grantly decided, "and I shall ask the Coopers to come, too. They never go anywhere, poor things."

Shortly after this, she fell asleep, Tejo curled on her lap. Senhor Tavares painted, Robert and Emma talked. He asked her to describe Gerald, and she tried, but it was a smudged sketch, and after a time she gave it up.

"He's not your type," she said. "He's hard-working and hates to waste time. He even works at his parties. What he'd make of you, spending most of your time basking, I can't imagine."

"It's this dual background I told you about. A father and mother with widely divergent ideas on upbringing. I was in a nice warm bath one minute, and shoved under a cold shower the next."

"If your mother was the warm bath one, she appears to have won the contest."

"You think so? I work hard in Melo's office. I run my three establishments efficiently—the one here, the one near Oporto and the one near Beja. I look after my land and make it productive. I look after my workers and my tenants. I'd like you to see how tough and competent I look riding round the countryside. I'd like to drive you to Beja and show you what I've achieved in the once-unirrigated earth. Swimming is only one of my accomplishments."

"Who won the religious contest?"

"My mother, of course. That was a prerequisite of the marriage. She was the only child of what she called saints from heaven and what my father labelled Holy Joes. Not a single embrace during the whole of their courtship, unless her father was standing by with a stop watch. No outings without a chaperone. No dancing except when her mother or her aunts got up little affairs at their houses. You'd have thought she would have enjoyed freedom after that, wouldn't you?"

"Didn't she?"

"Yes and no. She never understood women who opted out of the job of bringing up children. She thought it the highest privilege accorded to womankind."

"And do you?"

"Of course." He sounded surprised. "I like a nursery-soap smell about a house. Don't you?"

"Yes."

He rolled nearer and propped himself up on his elbows to study her.

"Tell me: speaking purely academically, don't you agree that you and I, without this apparently insurmountable barrier between us, would have made a perfect pair?"

"For a time," she said.

"Oh, you admit so much? What would happen after that time?"

"I'd get a guilt complex about leading such a heavenly life."

"I know. The English can't relax. If they're not keeping up with the latest political developments round the globe, if they're not victors over every last weed on the lawn, if they haven't sprayed the roses or helped with the bazaar or hosed the car or cleaned the shoes ready for tomorrow or attended the parent-teacher meeting or taken the things to the dry cleaners, they can't put their feet up. Their sense of duty is fantastic, and admirable, and very, very grim. I'm talking about my father's kind of English; they still exist and they're still bringing up their sons in the fine old traditions, and they're the salt of the earth, I'm not denying it, but I wish they wouldn't write off the people who enjoy leisure when they've got leisure. Do you think my father would have stretched out like me, purring in the sunshine? No. He would have considered it a kind of letting-go. 'A good, brisk swim, my boy, and then out you come and give me a hand with the mowing.' It's a kind of fear that they'll get a taste for lazing—like women who won't eat one rich cake in case they can't stop at one. Am I making sense?"

"Only half. Go on; it's soothing."

"Are you asleep?"

"Only half."

He bent over to see. Lady Grantly stirred and gave a gentle snore. Senhor Tavares walked backwards to view his canvas and stopped only just in time to prevent himself from falling into the water. His exclamation therefore seemed a natural one, so that it was some moments before Emma and Robert understood that it had been an exclamation of surprise, and that his eyes were still fixed, not on his work, but on the little gate that gave entrance to the pool. When they looked up at last, it was to see Gerald Delmont coming towards them.

Chapter 10

He spoke as he drew near, while Robert was getting to his feet and giving Emma his hand to pull her upright.

"I'm sorry to disturb you like this. They told me at the office in Sintra that Mr. Weybridge was working at his own house. You're Weybridge, I presume? How do you do? My name is Delmont. I won't kiss you, Emma; your face is wet. How do you do, Lady Grantly? I understood from a rather confused communication from Emma that you were ill."

It was plain that Lady Grantly thought she was having a disagreeable dream. When she spoke, it would have been difficult to detect any welcome in her tone.

"What in the world are you doing here?" she demanded.

"I came in an attempt to accomplish in person what telephone calls, letters and telegrams failed to do: find out exactly what has gone wrong with your title to the house, and take Emma home. I arrived by air two hours ago and I have bookings for us both on the night flight tomorrow. Between now and then, perhaps Mr. Weybridge would be so good as to give up some of his time to make the legal situation clear."

"Of course." It was Robert speaking in his most relaxed manner. "But not at once, surely? Have you had lunch?"

"I had the usual plastic food on the plane."

"Then sit down. You must be hot and tired."

He looked neither. Angry as she was at his arrogant manner, Emma conceded that nothing could have been more cool or more elegant than the clothes he was wearing. His fair, untanned skin made Robert's look almost black.

"Just a drink," he told Robert. "Then I must take Emma away; we have a lot to say to one another."

"This is Senhor Tavares," Lady Grantly said. "He is a very well-known artist and is kindly giving me lessons. Senhor Tavares, this is Mr. Delmont, the fiancé of Miss Challis."

Senhor Tavares gave one of his deepest bows. Gerald gave a nod.

"I am painting Miss Challis. It is a commission from Lady Grantly," Augusto said.

"Oh, really? I'm afraid there won't be time for any more sittings."

"No sittings," Augusto explained. "Here in the pool, in her costume for swimming, just as she is. It is a pity to take her away so soon. It will be a fine picture."

"I'm sure it would have been," Gerald said with a polite condescension worse than any insult, and which showed Emma how deeply angry he was. "But I'm afraid it must be put off. I sent you," he continued, turning to Emma, "two urgent telegrams which you didn't bother to reply to. I received a letter from Mr. Weybridge giving me a far from lucid account of a so-called claimant from Mozambique. It sounded to us in London as though the whole matter had been badly bungled, so I came out in the hope of getting a clearer picture. I went straight from the airport to Sintra and left my luggage at the hotel. I then went to Senhor Melo's office and was told that he was away, but that Mr. Weybridge had the matter in hand and was working on it at his home. I must say it looks very pleasant work."

There was a pause.

"Has he finished?" Lady Grantly asked icily.

"He's exhausted," Robert said in a kind, insufferably paternal tone. "All that rushing round in this hot weather. Sit down, Delmont. Beer? Chilled port? Campari with a dash—"

"Beer, please."

"It seems extraordinary," Lady Grantly said to Tejo, still curled up on her lap, "that anybody should come all this way just to be insulting and to spoil everybody's pleasure. Someone ought to tell Mr. Delmont that Robert is doing all he can for this poor woman, while I'm taking care of the children. I don't see what anybody could have done until those poor little things had been shod and clothed. Five of them, and only the youngest with a pair of shorts you could call whole."

"Do I understand that you're talking about the five children Mr. Weybridge mentioned in his letter?" Gerald asked her.

"Who else does he think I'm talking about?" she asked Robert angrily. "So thin! When I first saw them in that crate, all huddled together, I felt *ill*."

"Crate?" Gerald repeated in bewilderment.

"Tell him about the luggage crate, Emma," Lady Grantly requested. "Imagine coming out all this way when he hasn't taken in anything at all, even though he admits that Robert sent him a letter. Tell him that the crate wasn't nearly large enough for a mother and five children, however thin. And tell him about the servants being so unfriendly. Tell him there's nothing whatever he can do here. The thing is going to take years."

"That I can well believe," Gerald said, his eyes sweeping the scene. "Perhaps, Lady Grantly, you would be so kind as to address me directly?"

"Yes, I will." She gave an angry bounce and turned towards him. "I shall tell you that you have made me very angry, and I've no doubt it's bad for me, since I've not been well. The least you could have done was write to Emma and ask her to stay on here for a little while and look after me, instead of telling her in that schoolmaster way that you had her return reservation. We were all perfectly happy until you came walking in uninvited."

"I can see you were. But Emma has a great many things to see to in London. I might go as far as to point out that her duty to me comes before any duty you may feel she has towards you. Mr. Weybridge also has certain duties, which you pay him to do. I cannot see that lounging round a swimming pool is going to settle the not unimportant matter of a woman who is claiming half your house."

"You are almost as disagreeable a man as your father. More I cannot say," pronounced Lady Grantly.

Robert attempted to introduce a calmer note. "I've got some of the documents here, if you'd like to look at them," he told Gerald. "We could go to my study and—"

"I'd prefer the office, if it's all the same to you. You were going there some time this afternoon, I presume?"

"No."

"No?"

"No. You see, I work with Melo on a part-time basis, and I time the parts very carefully. If you insist, of course I'll stretch a point and meet you there in about an hour. Did you come out here in a taxi?"

"No. I hired a self-drive. Emma, if you'll change, we can go."

She turned pale. All eyes were resting expectantly upon her. She wanted, more than anything in the world, to refuse. He was alien, an interloper from that other world which had receded so far. He was out of his element and he had behaved in a sneering, insufferable way. But by challenging her to go with him, he had put himself into her hands. If she refused, he would have to walk away, through the little iron gateway, looking a fool and a beaten fool. She did not want to go with him, but she could not bring herself to humiliate him.

"I'll change in a minute," she said. "Senhor Tavares, do you want to put in some touches while I pose for you, for a change?"

"Thank you, thank you. If you will stand just as you are for a little while, it will help me."

Gerald turned to address Robert. "Is this claim, this woman's claim, going to stand up in court?" he enquired.

"If she makes a claim, I think it will."

"What do you mean by 'if'? Isn't that why she came to Portugal?"

"Not specifically. She came because she hoped to get some help from her brother-in-law, Manuel."

"The fellow who sold the house to Lady Grantly?"

"Yes. But he's in Angola. He left Portugal shortly after the sale of the house was concluded."

"Shouldn't that have alerted you? Suspicious, to say the least, skipping off like that."

"He'd been hoping to skip off to Angola for years. The

money he got for the house gave him a chance of buying a farm out there. His brother's widow came here because she knew that her children were entitled to a share of the house, but she had no ideas beyond that. She's been given living quarters in Senhor Tavares's house, and she's working for him. I sent one of the clerks from the office out to talk to her and make some notes, but I don't have to tell you that the whole thing is a mass, not to say mess, of complications."

"What steps have you taken with regard to this Manuel?"

"We've written to him, of course. When we've proof that he's received the letter, we'll wait and see how he reacts. If he does nothing, we'll ask a firm of lawyers in Luanda to send a man out to his farm and ask him to come to Luanda to discuss the matter."

"And if he won't?"

"He probably will. The Portuguese are rather fond of getting together for a discussion. It doesn't commit them to anything. Manuel will do a bit of probing to find out how valid the widow's claim is, and then he'll go home and think it over. If in the meantime the widow has decided to take action, she can go to the courts and ask for the sale—the sale of the house—to be declared null and void. Which would be the beginning of an indefinite amount of unscrambling."

"At the pace you're proceeding, I imagine the thing will take months."

"Years," Lady Grantly corrected. "So your absurd dash to, as it were, man the outposts looks a little ridiculous, don't you think? Nobody could have acted more promptly than Robert, or been more kind, and you should be grateful to him because he has looked after Emma while I wasn't well. You had no business to come rushing in, brandishing return tickets and not even taking the trouble to walk to the other side of the pool to see how Senhor Tavares was getting on with his picture of Emma. You're angry, of course, because she didn't leave me and go back to London, but if you'd been a man of feeling, you would have told Emma to stay with me and see me through this upsetting business of having to give up half my house."

"Even though the case might take years? Did you feel, perhaps, that I should have postponed our wedding?"

"You put it off without any kind of protest when your father asked you. He told me so himself. If you could oblige your father, Emma could have been allowed to help me. You may consider me a tiresome old woman, but I love Emma and I consider she's throwing herself away in insisting on marrying you. And that's the last word I shall utter on the subject, except to say that I've been against it all along, as you well know."

"As I well know," Gerald agreed. "Emma, go and change, will you?"

Robert saw them to the car. They left him standing in the courtyard, and some saving instinct kept Gerald silent as they drove to Sintra. Seated beside him, Emma fought to apply reason and bring her mind back to a state in which she could think clearly. Reason. Admit, first, the effect that Robert Weybridge had had on her. Was that to be wondered at? He had a splendid body, a good brain and a beguiling tongue. All that had happened was that she had allowed the combination of charm and country to swamp her. It had been a dream, and now Gerald was here and she was awake. She had licked off the jam and come to the plain bread and butter. Until she went up to Yorkshire and met Lady Grantly, she had been quite convinced that she was doing right in marrying Gerald; all she had to do now was convince herself that nothing had changed. She couldn't expect to live her whole life lying beside filtered pools and shading her eyes from the sun. That was all very well for a holiday, but it would soon pall. In London, she could build a good life; everything cultural was within reach, and she could go to new and provocative plays and watch television from midday to midnight if she wanted to. That was real life, not lying in the sunshine looking up at a steel-blue sky and trying out the wines of the district and eating figs straight off the tree and watching peasant girls drawing water from wells. That kind of life was demoralizing. You went to seed. You rotted.

Reason—that was the thing.

Reason upheld her until she and Gerald were seated in the garden of his hotel having tea.

"I'm surprised to have you to myself at last," he observed. "I began to think you wouldn't be able to extricate yourself."

"From what?"

"The party at the pool. How much of that fellow have you been seeing?"

"Senhor Tavares?"

"Don't try sarcasm, for God's sake. When I came out here, I expected to have to fight Lady Grantly for possession of my fiancée. What I didn't expect was to find my fiancée lying in the arms of a half-naked fellow who's supposed to be protecting Lady Grantly's interests. How much time has he been spending with you?"

"All he can."

"I'm not the jealous type—you know that."

"What have you had to be jealous about?"

"That's what makes it so hard to understand. This change in you I'm talking about. Until you went up on that blasted trip to Yorkshire, I at least knew you—or thought I did. You came down announcing that you'd found an outlet for your nursing instincts, and you threw all our plans in the air and came out here. And stayed out here. So the question now arises: did you put off your trip home because Lady Grantly had taken to her bed, or because Weybridge was anxious to take you to his?"

"How long do you think you'll take to work out the answer?"

"I'll know the answer tomorrow night. If you get on that plane with me, I'll acknowledge that I was misled by the evidence of my eyes, and I'll apologize. You either come with me or you don't. It's as simple as that."

"Good. Isn't it time you went to the office?"

"Yes, it is." He asked the waiter for the bill. "I'll be glad to get out of this heat. I hope you won't be too sorry to leave."

"So do I."

"Are you trying to tell me something?"

"Yes. I love Portugal and I wish I didn't have to leave it."

"My dear girl, if you lived out here, you'd be sick of it in three months."

"What would I be sick of?"

"The lack of intellectual stimulation. The tourist atmosphere. The tax-dodgers. It's a backwater, when all's said and done, and you're too vital to enjoy being in a backwater for long. Who would you meet here except a succession of Lady Grantlys? What would you do when the sun-bathing season was over? You can meet more people who matter at one of the parties I give than you could come across in a year out here. If this bunch of expatriates ever did anything, they're certainly not doing it any longer. If they ever did any work, they've retired. If they ever knew anything about the arts, they've forgotten it. They're living in a state of suspended animation, waiting for the time to come for their next visit home. Don't you agree?"

"Don't you agree that you're behaving very oddly for a man who's been away from his fiancée for some weeks?"

"You're forgetting that I walked in on a scene which most fiancés might have misconstrued."

"So I am."

"I've made you angry, but that's not a bad thing if it helps you to pull yourself together. You've had a good holiday, but it's over; now let's get back to work and start living normally again." He rose. "How are you going to put in the time while I'm in the office?"

"If you'll let me take the car, I'll go back to Lady Grantly's. I'll call for you at about six-thirty and drive you out."

"Out where?"

"Surely you're going to spend some time at Lady Grantly's?"

"I am going to spend as little time there as possible. I'm tired of being abused. There's no point in your going back now; you can do a bit of shopping and choose something we can take back for my father and one or two other people. When I'm finished with the office, we'll have a drink and dine somewhere, here or in Lisbon, whichever you prefer."

Robert's car was outside the office, but she did not see him, either then or when Gerald joined her just before seven o'clock. The evening went better than she had expected; they had both had time to simmer down, and they were both on their guard and anxious to avoid a repetition of the afternoon's argument. Their conversation was almost exclusively of the houses in London that he had looked at, the furniture he planned to buy and the various makes of small cars available to provide a second one for her use. She gave her mind firmly to what he was saying, made sensible suggestions and responded with a warmth sufficient to reassure him, though she found it impossible to respond when he drove her back to Lady Grantly's at midnight and took her into an uncharacteristically passionate embrace.

"Tired?" he asked.

"No."

"Can you go in and get me your return ticket and your passport? I'll need them when I confirm the booking."

She brought them out to him.

"Are you coming to wish Lady Grantly a happy birthday tomorrow?" she asked.

"I'll send some flowers. Are you quite determined to go on that silly fire-watching expedition?"

"It's not an expedition. We're simply walking down to the village after dinner, that's all."

"Well, mind you walk back in time to be ready when I call for you. I'll be here just before midnight."

She stood at the gate watching him as he drove away. Then she turned towards the house—and found Robert Weybridge beside her.

"Not a sound!" he ordered melodramatically. "And no calling for help. Where can we talk?"

"We can't."

"Don't thwart me. You can't thwart a man who's just had to stand by watching another man embracing the woman he loves. Come on—we'll go and sit in my car. It's hidden in the Coopers' pine wood."

"Haven't you any—"

"—scruples? No. I thought you were never coming. I began to imagine the worst, but I comforted myself by remember-

ing what a cold fish he looked. He'd obviously warmed up a
bit by the end of the evening. One minute more, and I'd
have crawled out of the bushes and lifted him up by his wild
silk shirt and dropped him over the cliff. Get in."

Seated beside her, he wasted no time on preliminaries.

"You can't do it, Emma," he said firmly.

"Do . . ."

"Don't pretend. You know quite well what I mean. You
can't marry him. You'd be out of your mind. So would he, if
it comes to that. You're about as well suited as a . . . a robin
and a vulture. You've got to give him back his expensive
ring and tell him he can get a rebate on the return booking
he made for you. You'll never make a pair. What got you
into it in the first place, for God's sake?"

"Love, I suppose. There's more than one kind."

"Only one kind makes a marriage. Your trouble is that
you're sorry for him. Why, I can't imagine. There was some
basis for your excess of protectiveness in the case of Lady
Grantly—but this man? Emma, you've got to tell him."

"Tell him what?"

"You've got to tell him—if you won't, I will—that you and
I are in love. You've got to . . . Are you crying?"

"A bit. Don't stop me. I'm . . . I'm so tired."

"My poor, misguided, idiotic darling. If you're crying for
that man, don't. He's got enough self-love to keep him going
until he meets the next girl who's sorry for him. Want a nice,
clean hankie?"

"Yes, please. He's . . . he's all right. You saw him at his worst
this morning. Underneath, he's—"

"—just a simple, homely, shy sort of chap? Oh, Emma,
grow up! You're just the last dying flicker of his past—his pre-
London past. We all cling to our beginnings for a time. He

belongs to his world and you belong to mine. Will you tell him, or will I?"

"You don't understand. I *know* him. He *knows* me."

"And that makes you feel nice and safe?"

"In a way."

"Are you going to argue that, loving me—which you do—you can't feel safe because you don't know enough about me?"

"I'm trying to say that if a girl agrees to marry a man she's known all her life, and then goes away on a brief holiday and meets another man and in three weeks decides that he's the one she really wants, then she's . . ."

"Well, what? Unstable?"

"Yes. She's giving up something she knows, someone she knows, to . . ."

"To take a chance with someone she doesn't know, but loves? Do you know why you agreed to marry Delmont? Because he was a bloodless type who never plunged deep enough to look for any answering passion in you. If he had, you would have realized that he was incapable of arousing it. You don't need security—you're the sort of woman who dispenses it. You need a man who'll love you, not a man who'll look after you. You need children born out of nights of passion, not family planning. You need someone who can live and love and laugh. You need me. Do you love me?"

"You've said so, several times."

"Do you?"

"Yes."

"Then what are you afraid of?"

"Making a fool of myself. Sending Gerald away and finding out that what he says is true—that this life isn't the real me."

"What does that matter? Stick to essentials. You and I love one another. You know as much about me, fundamentally, as you know about Delmont. You know about his personal habits, maybe, but you don't know and you won't know the essential man until you're married to him. That's what I like about marriage—its challenge. You're given, each of you, a ticket marked Love, and if you're lucky, it takes you all the way. It took my parents all the way. What did they know about one another when they left the church they were married in? Nothing, nothing, nothing. You have to be married, and then you find out. You don't find out merely by living together, because the gate's always open and that's no good. You have to hold your hands out and get them manacled, and after that the fun begins. Marry me, and I'll prove it. Tell him it's off, Emma."

"No. Not yet. Robert, let me do this my way, please. Please!"

"What's your way?"

"Let me go back with him to England. Let me tell him, shortly after we get there, that I'm not going to marry him. Let me come back here and stay with Lady Grantly and see you—"

"Wait. If you want to go back with him, then do. I think you're wrong, and it's crazy, but if you want to do it that way, I won't stop you. But when you come back, you come back to marry me. Off the plane and into the church."

"Catholic Church?"

"Naturally. Do you mind?"

"No. I don't care what you are."

"Thank you. May I ask what you are, if anything?"

"Church of England."

"Pass, friend."

He held her gently. With her head on his shoulder, she wept a little and then was still. They heard the wind in the trees, the sigh of the sea. The darkness wrapped them round. And for the first time since she had left her grandparents' home, she felt secure—and at peace.

Chapter
11

"Of course you're wrong," Lady Grantly said the next morning, "and Robert is an angel to let you go. You're very selfish not to think of him. You're still concerned with the feelings of that other man—and what concern did he show for our feelings when he made his way into Robert's garden and began to bully everybody? The thing to do is give him back his ring and send him away. If it's going to hurt him, which I doubt, because he's got no proper feelings, it won't hurt less for being said or done in England. But it's my birthday, and thank you for my lovely palette, and look at Robert's lovely flowers—Gerald Delmont sent some too, by the way; why did you tell him it was my birthday? Senhor Tavares gave me these two beautiful paint brushes. And the Coopers—you told the Coopers, too."

"Yes. I thought they'd feel we were being friendly. Is that their parcel?"

"Yes. It's a birthday cake, which makes it very awkward, because the maids brought me one as soon as I was dressed, all done with icing and little pearly balls. We might cut the Cooper cake at tea time and put the other out at dinner, don't you think?"

"No. Other way round. I think Robert would enjoy Mrs. Cooper's cake more than the other one."

"Then that's what we'll do. I've got three bottles of champagne—two at dinner, I thought, and the other to drink just before you go off with that man."

"What's for dinner?"

"It's a surprise. Now go and tell Lourdes I want her," Lady Grantly said.

When the guests were assembled in the drawing room before dinner, she made an announcement.

"When we've dined, and while we're waiting to go out and see the Saint Anthony fires," she said, "I'm going to get out my cards and put a little question to them."

"Cards?" Senhor Tavares looked blank.

"Ordinary playing cards. I just lay them out in a certain order, and the answer is always right. They brought me quite a lot of money once."

"The cards did?" Senhor Tavares said wistfully. "That was very fortunate. Are you going to make some more money come?"

"No. I am going to satisfy myself that Emma is going to marry a dark man and not a fair one."

"But he is fair. I saw, at the pool, that he was fair."

"You also heard, at the pool, that I don't care for him. I won't make a secret of the fact that I think she's going to marry Robert."

"Marry Robert!" Senhor Tavares seized Robert's hands and wrung them. "Roberto, such news!"

"Wait," said Lady Grantly. "Emma insists on going back to England with Mr. Delmont, just to make sure."

"Make sure of what?" Augusto asked in bewilderment.

"Make sure she doesn't want him. So I want to be reassured by the cards."

"So do I," said Robert. "How soon do we begin? Are those the cards over there?"

"Yes, but we shall dine first. Then the cards. It won't take long; just a simple question, fair or dark?"

"Do they talk?" Robert asked.

"If the knave of spades comes up, it's the dark man she's going to marry. If the knave of hearts comes up, it's the fair man."

"What about the two other knaves?" Robert asked.

"I remove those. Now we shall go and dine."

There was clear soup of no very definite flavour, a whole fish decorated with a beetroot spine, tomato fins and black olive eyes, and a tender but tasteless round of steak surrounded by an array of vegetables so elaborately arranged that the meat had cooled in the process. The peach flambée was pretty to look at but tasted woody. At the end of the meal, Lady Grantly admitted that she had perhaps asked too much of her staff. But Mrs. Cooper's cake was beyond criticism, and Senhor Tavares endeared himself to her by eating four thick slices.

The men were left at the table, and Lady Grantly led the ladies to her bedroom. Then they joined the men, who were in the drawing room, and Lady Grantly took up her pack of cards, removed them from their case and gave them to Mrs. Cooper.

"Don't let me see; just remove the knave of diamonds and the knave of clubs," she asked her. "Thank you. Now give the cards back to me, face downwards. Now I shall simply lay them out in rows, and the first knave to appear is the one."

About halfway through the pack, when tension among the spectators was mounting, the knave of spades appeared.

"You see?" Lady Grantly held it up in triumph, and gave a deep sigh of thankfulness. "They're never, never wrong."

"Don't you ever cheat?" Robert asked.

"Never. Now I'm quite happy. I feel much better. Robert, when are we going out to look at the fires?"

"Do you feel like walking as far as the village? It's more fun if we walk."

"I feel up to anything. Shall we go?"

"In a little while. It's a bit light still."

They allowed darkness to fall before setting out. They had to pass Emma's suitcases, which had been put in the hall, and a slight gloom fell on the company. Lady Grantly went first with Mr. Cooper; Senhor Tavares escorted Mrs. Cooper, and Emma and Robert brought up the rear.

It was a beautiful night, clear and warm. There were several little fires along the way, each surrounded by groups of young people. In the village there was a more ambitious blaze onto which children piled more and more wood, while the old people watched indulgently from open doorways. Robert allowed Emma to watch for a time and then drew her away.

"We haven't long," he said. "Just time enough to show you something."

He led her along the street and stopped before the village chapel. He opened the door and ushered her in.

"Like it?" he asked. "My mother had it built. There's a little cross outside with her name on it, but she didn't die here. She died in the quinta up north. But this is where I'd like us to be married, if you agree."

"I . . . I'd love it," she said shakily. "Oh, Robert, I'll come back soon, I promise!"

"A good place to make a vow," he said, and led her outside. "When you've gone, I'll come back and watch the fires and think about you. All night. They'll keep this up all night. After midnight, they'll roast fresh sardines and hand out wine. Do you know what all those little altars in the doorways are?"

"I know they're made by the children."

"There's a chapel in Lisbon which is said to be built over the room in which Saint Anthony was born—Lisbon's patron saint. He was only called Saint Anthony of Padua because he died there. He was born in Lisbon. The money for the church that was built in the eighteenth century was collected by children; they made little altars like these and put them on the doorsteps of their homes. Nice idea, don't you think? Look, there's Maria."

"I saw her with the children at one of the fires. Robert, don't you think she's lovely? Not just pretty; lovely. Surely some man in the village will—"

"I hope not. It would ruin my hopes. Do you know where those two snaps are?"

"The ones you took at Augusto's?"

"Yes. They're on their way to Mozambique."

She paused and turned to look at him. "I don't understand."

"It's a gesture of hope. I knew, everybody knew that the two brothers, Manuel and Duarte, were always quarrelling. And we all knew what they quarrelled over. Women. But I remembered something else: that the reason they quarrelled was because they always wanted the same woman. If a woman appealed to Manuel, she invariably appealed to Duarte, and vice versa. Are you reading me, Challis?"

"I am. Go on."

"So when I sent the official letter to Manuel, telling him about the widow's claims, I put in a brief note of my own. Don't worry, I said to him, about the woman; she is being cared for and so are the children, and as she is very beautiful—see snapshot enclosed—it is likely that some man will soon wish to marry her."

"Do you think—"

"Cross your fingers. If she appealed to Duarte, I'll bet you one hundred escudos that Manuel will take a look at that snap and see a way out of his difficulty. How about that for astuteness?"

"You really think he'll come and—"

"Come? No. But I think he'll send for them. The lovely Maria and the children. In which case all settlements will be made under the eye of the lawyers in Luanda, and I shall be free to go back to my carefree splashings by the pool."

"Did you mention this to Gerald?"

"Are you crazy? Why would I mention it to Gerald? Would it have made him cry, as it's made you? No. He would have had me certified, or struck off the lawyers' lists or something of that kind—unprofessional behaviour. And now we've got to go back to the house and I've got to stand aside and watch you going away with another man. Lady Grantly said it might do me good—stiffen me. What did she mean by that?"

"That your moral fiber would grow as strong as mine. Oh, Robert . . ."

"All right. Say it."

"I love you."

"I know. What greater proof could I have than seeing you

depart with a man whose ring you're still wearing? God grant me patience. That's the prayer I prayed in that chapel."

They arrived to find the others in the drawing room, awaiting Gerald's arrival. He drove up at midnight, calm and efficient, and carrying a light three-quarter-length coat. He threw it across a chair in the drawing room, bowed to Lady Grantly and nodded to the others.

"Your passport, Emma," he said.

He picked up his coat and from one of the pockets extracted his own and Emma's passports, and their air tickets.

"There's not much point in giving them to me now," Emma pointed out. "Keep them until we get to the airport."

"Very well." He replaced passports and tickets in the pocket of his coat and laid it down. "We haven't long, I'm afraid."

"Long enough to drink a toast," Robert said. "Lady Grantly saved some of the birthday champagne."

"It's too late, I'm afraid, to wish you many happy returns," Gerald said, and a gleam in his eye showed that the ambiguity of the remark was not unintentional. "It's after midnight."

"Will you open the bottle, Robert?" Lady Grantly asked.

He filled their glasses and then held up his own to Emma.

"Happy return," he said. "And a long and happy married life."

They all drank. After one sip, Robert turned and walked slowly out onto the terrace and spoke over his shoulder.

"Come and look at the view. It's never looked better."

They came one by one, glasses in hand. Then the glasses were left empty, on the table that stood on the terrace or on one of the tables in the drawing room. Lady Grantly went to her room to get the list of books she wanted Emma to order in England. Mr. Cooper fetched his wife's handbag, Senhor Tavares went to get his theatrical evening cloak. They made their farewells. Only Robert remained.

"Well, I'm the last," he said. "Goodbye, Delmont. Emma, I think I might be allowed to kiss you goodbye."

It was a brief, light kiss dropped on her cheek. As Robert drew back, there was a sharp exclamation from Gerald.

"What the hell . . ."

He had picked up his coat. On the floor beside it, two air tickets were lying—but only one passport.

He picked them up and felt in his pocket. Then he felt in all his other pockets. His movements became more and more rapid and agitated; he dropped the coat and began to search the floor.

"Your passport. Emma's passport. It's dropped out. Look for it, Emma, for God's sake; don't just stand there. We're late as it is, blast it, with all this champagne and farewells." He stood still and gazed wildly round. "It was here. I had it. I had both passports. I took them out—you saw them. Are you sure you didn't take yours?"

"Quite sure. Has it got tucked into a corner of your pocket?"

Five minutes' intensive search by all four—Emma and Gerald, Lady Grantly and Robert—established the fact that the passport was not in the coat pockets and not in the room. The search, extended to the hall and to the terrace, produced nothing.

"I don't understand!" Gerald shouted, beside himself with agitation and rage. "I had the thing here. You all saw it. You all . . ." He stopped abruptly. "Someone's taken it," he ended grimly. "That's the only possible explanation. Someone has taken it."

"Nonsense," Lady Grantly said sharply. "Who could use somebody else's passport?"

"They could use it to prevent her from travelling, couldn't they?" Gerald asked, swinging round to confront her. "I see it all now. With her passport, she could go with me. Without it, she couldn't. And you"—he turned to Robert and spoke with no attempt to mask his hatred—"you're the one with the most interest in keeping her here. Hand it over, d'you hear? I give you one minute to produce it. You can't deny that you've taken it, can you? You came in here when we were all on the terrace, didn't you? You sneaked back here and took it. Come on, hand it over."

Robert spread his hands helplessly. "You may search me," he said.

"Search you? I'll—"

"He wasn't the only one who came into this room," Emma pointed out. "Mr. Cooper came in. So did Senhor Tavares."

"What interest would they have in keeping you here? Who else but . . . Unless," he ended slowly, and with mounting conviction, "it was you."

"Do you think I'd go to your pocket and take my passport out of it?"

"Yes, I do."

"Do you know what you're saying?"

"Certainly I know. I'm saying that you wanted to find a way out of going back to England, without the bother of explanations and fuss. My advice to you is to hand me back that passport and let's see if we can catch that plane. If you won't give it back, I won't wait for you."

"I haven't got it."

"You're not a very convincing liar."

"If I'd taken it, I would give it back after that," Emma said.

"You needn't wait for me."

They looked at one another.

"I see," Gerald said slowly. "I was a fool to come out. No. I was a fool to let you come out."

He turned and walked out of the house. They heard the car engine roar, and a few moments later the sound died away in the distance.

Lady Grantly was the first to break the silence. "Such a pity it's past midnight," she said musingly.

"Why?" Robert asked.

"Because I couldn't have had a nicer birthday present. Robert, why don't you go home? Let Emma rest. You can see her from tomorrow to the end of your days."

"I'll go presently," he said. "Go to bed and I'll go home when I've said good night to Emma."

It was not a long good night. They agreed later that, absorbed though they were in one another, they could not have failed to hear sounds in the hall, if there had been sounds. They heard none. But when they walked to the door to go out to Robert's car, Emma's passport was lying on the hall table.

And beside it lay the knave of hearts.

A Note About the Author

Born and brought up in India, Elizabeth Cadell was educated in Calcutta, London, and Darjeeling. She started writing in 1947 and since then has published twenty-five novels including *The Golden Collar* (1968) and *The Past Tense of Love* (1969). Mrs. Cadell now lives in Portugal.